Chaos Magic

I0715883

Chaos Magic

CHAOS MAGIC (c) 2025 by JEN KNOX
All Rights Reserved

No part of this book may be used or reproduced in any manner whatsoever without permission except in the case of brief quotations embodied in critical essays or reviews.

This is a work of the author's imagination. Any references to historical events, real people, or real places are used fictitiously. Other names, characters, places, and events are products of the author's imagination, and any resemblance to actual events or places or persons, living or dead, is entirely coincidental.

Attention schools and businesses; for discounted copies on large orders please contact the publisher directly.

Kallisto Gaia Press Inc.
PO Box 220
Davilla TX 76523 info@kallistogaiapress.org
(254) 654-7205

Edited by: Tony Burnett
Author's Photo: Sarah Henderson Cover Design: Christopher J. Shanahan

ISBN: 978-1-952224-43-0

Distributed by Ingram Lightning Source

Chaos Magic

a novel

Jen Knox

Also by Jen Knox

We Arrive Uninvited
The Glass City

After the Gazebo

Sections

for those who leave space for magic

The Lavender Center

The **Lavender Center claimed to be** an empowering sanctuary for domestic abuse and trafficking survivors. Those who suffered mentally or physically could show up at the door, bedraggled and fearful, only to leave ready to take on the world. So said the website. Lissa tried to smile at the unlikely but comforting promise, but pain radiated along her jaw. *He stole my smile.* She prepared herself for what her mother would say about the place.

The residence's tagline was "Holistic Healing by All Means Necessary." But unlike most rehabilitation centers in the area, TLC did not offer psychological counseling or tech-supported treatment plans, and residents had to sign a twenty-page document that explained exactly why the therapies provided did not claim to be medicinal. Accordingly, TLC was classified as a retreat instead of a rehabilitation center, and it seemed to be targeting wealthier abuse victims as opposed to out-of-work substitute teachers like Lissa.

The reviews on Google were mixed. The most scathing said, "The owners have a clear disregard for good, Christian values," "Devil's work!" and "Lavender whatever is full of woo-woo. I couldn't even make it a week before I hauled ass outta there." The best reviews included passages such as "My entire life changed in a month, and I finally realized my true worth. Who knew that getting beat up by a shithead would lead to the best experience of my entire life," and "I'm sixty-seven years old, and I feel like I finally have a fresh start! My life is worth fighting for." The only neutral review read, "I broke the bank to get there, but it was worth it. I know women who aren't flush with cash could benefit from these services."

Lissa's finger hovered above the call button. She imagined her mother's response. A retired clinical psychiatrist and researcher, Pauline would not let Lissa hear the end of this. But there was no one else to call. She glanced at herself in the mirror, allowing her dark hair to cover most of her face. It almost hid the bruising.

Not long before Lissa ended up in the hospital, Trent had

started insisting she join him at a church the size of an outdoor mall. He knew she wasn't religious in that way—neither was he, as far as she knew—but the preacher was locally famous for his intense charisma and archaic messaging. During one of the sermons, after telling the congregation that the etymology of women reminds us that a woman's duty is to be the wife of man, w/o-man, the preacher scanned the congregation and said that there were real women in the world, and there were those who were brainwashed into believing they needed to fill a man's role, and while he knew most in the congregation were true women, there were probably a few in this very room who needed to repent.

"Jesus will save you if you repent now," he'd said. "If you don't repent, you'll burn. A good woman knows her place." When Lissa stood up to leave, Trent's face grew red and he pulled her back down, hard.

"Don't embarrass me," he'd said between gritted teeth. That night the two argued until Lissa heard her voice fading to nothing. A whisp. Fading to nothing had been her pattern until the docility led to a sliced jaw. Imagining her tailbone hitting the slick pew beneath her as he pulled her down that day, Lissa lifted her hand to her face and traced the raised area that was still healing from the wound. She continued scrolling through the comments. "This place is full of witch-craft" seemed better than any religious alternative.

Shortly after withdrawing all her money from a small personal account and reluctantly cashing a check for the difference from Pauline, Lissa inventoried all her things that remained in the three-story house Trent still owned, a house that she would refuse to fight for. She began shoving clothes, her father's journals, a phone charger, a box of fruit bars, granola, and contact solution into a few bags to take off for the outskirts of Cleveland, Ohio with a $7,000 check.

Lissa had no energy, no other money, and very little hope aside from what her mother deemed a childish sort of magical thinking. With few friends at the time, thanks to her dormant life with Trent, coupled with the pandemic, she wished she still had people to call, to vent to. Though she'd pressed charges, and Trent had been arrested without question, his family was well off enough that Lissa worried he'd make bail, and she couldn't be anywhere near the neighborhoods she knew when that happened.

"And you're absolutely sure you don't want to try a more traditional option, with a firmly scientific grasp on the human mind?"

Pauline asked as Lissa zipped her backpack.

"Mom. I'll call an Uber."

"Fine, fine. It's fine," Pauline sighed, nudging her oversized glasses up her thin nose. "Here, let me help you."

Two hours later, Pauline and Lissa arrived at the front door of a large mansion in the middle of the woods in a newly dirt-covered Subaru. They sat in silence for a moment before Pauline reached for her daughter's hand. She started to say something, but Lissa interrupted, holding up her hand, "I'd like to go in by myself," Lissa said, giving her mother a gentle kiss on the cheek. "Thank you for driving me."

"Of course but let me get your bags out of the trunk," Pauline said with a pained expression. "Hey, if you get panicked, remember to count backwards. Slowly. Remind yourself you are safe."

"Thanks, Mom."

Lissa hesitated at the front door, conscious of her fresh scars. Just as she was about to ring the doorbell, the heavy wood door opened, and she was greeted by a woman in head-to-toe white who curtsied to Lissa, and then waved to Pauline. Lissa fought the urge to glance back or decode what a curtsy might mean, worried she might be tempted to run back to the car. She felt a wave and heard the whisper-song of her great-grandmother, whose voice she hadn't heard for years. *"Yooehr mahther's right. This is yer new start."* Lissa steadied herself, remembering her father's words from so many years ago, *allow yourself a little magic,* before taking a step inside. Lissa wanted more than a little.

"Come in, my dear. Lissa, correct?" the woman said. Everything about her was gentle and soft. The house, too, was warm, and though it was large, there was a coziness to it.

"Yes." Lissa glanced around the woman and down a long hallway that was bookended by two flights of stairs. She wanted to know the history of the house and could only imagine the spirits that must occupy it.

"You spoke with my partner, Glenda. I'm Doreen. Do you have a cellphone?"

"Glinda?" Lissa said, imagining a blonde materializing in a puffy pink dress and tall crown. She held tight to her phone.

"No, Glenda. She gets that a lot." She nodded toward the phone.

Lissa worried Doreen would take it from her. Instead, she held out a laminated sheet of paper with a QR code that ran down TLC's offerings, including reiki, shamanic healing, akashic record retrieval, hypnotherapy, yoga, life coaching, hydrotherapy, massage, heat therapy, therapeutic dance, somatic breathwork, and weekly treks to a salt cave to detox with a gong bath. There were also past life regressions and tuning fork sessions, which took place on a first-come, first-serve basis.

"All our residents' rooms are this way," she said, gesturing toward the right. "And our treatments are offered on the other side, though many of our offerings take place in the courtyard and outdoors as well. I'll give you a tour." Doreen's small, soft face seemed eternally kind, as though physically unable not to smile.

"It's beautiful," Lissa said.

"Are you hungry?"

"Honestly, I'm exhausted. I just want to rest today," Lissa said.

"Indeed! How about you try out the meditation room before we fully check you in? It's a good first stop. I see you already paid the deposit online. Do you happen to have a check for the balance?"

Lissa pulled the neatly folded check out of the back pocket of her jeans and handed it to the woman. "I hope this is everything."

"Perfect. Follow me." They walked down the hall and past a room on the right that contained a few residents in workout clothes who were whispering, likely about Lissa, and toward a curve along the narrow hallway. The house looked large from the outside, but it felt like a maze. Lissa wondered what was upstairs. They passed multiple rooms with bright doors and muraled walls that depicted the tree of life and images of goddesses from around the world. Doreen paused at a nondescript white door. "There are different tracks you can set on the keypad here on the wall, just as there are outside all the doors. I recommend the grounding meditation for new arrivals but go with your heart. We'll have your room ready when you're done." Doreen seemed to float as she led Lissa inside the all-white room with purple cushions. It was small—private but not claustrophobic. "You can leave the door cracked if you'd feel more comfortable that way. No one will bother you, but I'll be just down the hall and to the right. Four doors down."

Lissa nodded, wishing she could just go to her room and curl up in bed, but maybe this would help. She was willing to try anything. She closed the door gently, selected music randomly, and sat in the middle of the room, wishing she could feel something, anything. After a few minutes, she closed her eyes and prayed that she would feel some semblance of who she used to be—that anything here would work—as she focused on her breath. She still felt numb twenty minutes later, and a gentle shift in music signaled the end of the session. It was as though she'd simply lost time, and the only thing she felt was somewhat sleepier.

Doreen was waiting outside the door when Lissa emerged. "Cucumber and lemon infused," she said, handing Lissa a glass of water. "Would you like to meet the other residents today?"

"I'd really like to turn in for the day, to be honest." Lissa took a sip of the cool water.

"I completely understand. It's okay to feel overwhelmed and tired when you arrive. Breakfast is at 7 a.m. I understand that's a bit early for some, but I ask that you try your best to show up. Our goal at The Lavender Center is to help you rebuild yourself mind, body, and spirit. Research shows that an early riser is more likely to feel a sense of accomplishment by the end of each day."

Lissa imagined her mother questioning everything this woman said, asking for the source of the research on early risers and spending the rest of the night seeking contrary evidence, but Lissa just nodded. Doreen checked her tablet and asked, "What sound would you like to wake up to? Crickets, waves, Gregorian chanting, birdsong, classical, the gong, or …?"

"Waves. And I'm an early riser anyway—at least I used to be, before the pandemic."

"The pandemic, yes. It impacted us all so profoundly, my dear. Now if you don't mind, I have a welcome packet to email to you that includes a few short surveys, including food preferences. If you could fill that out before you turn in for the evening, I'd appreciate it. All the food is farm to table, and we have options for just about any allergy, but a little prep time is always nice."

"Thank you, Doreen." Lissa tried to smile with the half of her face that allowed it, wincing at the pain.

"Here you are," Doreen said, extending her arm and showing the slightest hint of a hand peeking out that led the way to a two-bed room with a large window that faced a courtyard at the side of the mansion. Outside, there was a ledge big enough for Lissa to sit on, and a small pond that Doreen said was home to a particularly majestic heron. "You'll be by yourself for a few days, then we expect another woman will be joining you. Her name is Annika. We don't usually get check-ins with such advance notice, but everyone's story is different."

Lissa wasn't exactly sure what Doreen meant, but she nodded. After Doreen left, Lissa filled out the surveys that asked about her overall contentment, anxiety levels, and belief systems. She hesitated on the food survey. Though a year ago, she wouldn't be able to imagine giving up so much as pork, Lissa checked Pescetarian on the preference sheet and hit submit. For the first time, she wondered if it was possible to do as her mother had suggested and hit the reset button on life. That night, she slept deeper than she had in years.

TLC: Week 2

After trying various therapies and hearing tear-filled stories with intermittent rage responses that came out in group sessions, Lissa still couldn't shake the numbness she'd felt since leaving home. There had been a few glimmers of sensation, almost like presence, but they faded as quickly as they arrived. At breakfast, the residents were introduced to the co-owner and original founder of The Lavender Center, Glenda.

"I aspire to bring you the magic of reacquainting with yourself."

Glenda had wavy gray hair that was twisted away from her face and secured with a silver clip. Her eyes were a shade lighter and two shades bluer than her hair, and her skin looked ageless. She spoke in a measured voice, the way Lissa used to speak to the parents of kids who had been caught vandalizing school property or bullying.

"The holistic healing world is complex and dynamic. There is no one right answer, and there are always new and better combinations of therapies coming into being as scientific discoveries intersect with spiritual exploration. I've been away for a month, traveling and speaking with healers from around the world." Glenda glanced around the table. "While I hated to be away, I am excited to bring to you what we've learned and to get to know those of you I was unable to greet. So let's do a check-in. Going around the table today, let me know your name and a single word that describes how you feel. No wrong answers."

"Marc. Enthused!" The slender man, who'd introduced himself to Lissa on her second day, seemed unable to sit still. His leg always bounced when he sat, and his jaw moved as though he was perpetually chewing. Lissa had actively avoided him because he was loud and unable to read social cues when people wanted to leave a conversation. He shook his head slightly from side to side and smiled with a faux shyness. "Mostly because you're back, Glenda."

Glenda offered him a courtesy smile and gestured to the next person. "And you, dear?"

"Bee. Defeated."

"Amber. Hungry. Mad. Fat."

"One word, Amber."

"Fat."

Glenda looked at Lissa.

"Lissa," Lissa said, hoping a word would come. "Numb."

"You're new. If you feel up to it, hang out after breakfast. I'd love to chat."

The rest of the residents, less than a dozen, all offered words that Lissa didn't hear, but she looked at each and nodded as though she did. Doreen concluded the circle with "Grateful," and then went back to retrieve and pass out covered dishes, each of which bore a resident's name.

Lissa lifted her lid to find what looked like an egg white omelet with spinach, tomatoes, and basil inside. There was wheat toast with marmalade and a mug of frothed almond chai. She looked at the courtesy list of ingredients and saw "eggs" = mung beans + nutritional yeast. She took a hesitant bite. The spices danced around her mouth, almost helping her to feel something, and she got a flash of her father sitting at the table at breakfast before one of his bike races, explaining that calories didn't count if you were an athlete as he devoured half a loaf of buttered wheat bread to carb-load.

"He's fell o' shite," her great-grandmother's voice would sometimes say to her, and she'd wondered if her father heard it, too. They weren't allowed to talk about it in front of anyone else, but he'd wink.

Lissa would laugh and dare her father to eat one more piece, which he would do, puffing his cheeks out like a chipmunk, feigning an overfullness that he never seemed to feel. "No. More. Room," he'd say, then pretend to topple over. She felt a rush of melancholy at the memory.

Marc bombarded Glenda with questions during breakfast as the rest of the residents listened to her answers about the various crystal, sound, and mushroom therapies she'd studied over the last month. He also asked her about reintegration because he was set to leave in a few days. In response, she placed her hand on the crown of his head like he was a child and told him to close his eyes.

"You're almost ready," she said.

This shut him up. As Doreen began clearing away plates,

mugs, and smoothie glasses, Glenda wandered over to Lissa and sat a comfortable distance away, which Lissa was glad for. Everyone cleared out, even Marc—after Doreen politely excused him. Lissa shifted in her chair. She wasn't entirely sure she bought into all this.

Glenda leaned in slightly, and Lissa got the whiff of lilac. "Numbness is normal. It's a freeze response, like the gazelle."

"I appreciate that. But it feels like I'm not living at all, not as a gazelle or anything."

"All of that will soon change," she said with maternal warmth. "You are perfectly fine, and we can support you."

"I have nightmares," Lissa admitted. She'd woken herself up screaming or sweating more than once.

"They're just the fear working itself out. You're getting re-united with your magic, sweetheart. If you don't feel it yet, you will. Annika will be good for you, I promise. And she'll be okay with the nightmares." She glanced at her phone, scrolling for a while. "Doreen has done an excellent job of scheduling you, but you've been here long enough that I'd like to adjust your routine and, if you're open to it, per-haps integrate some additional therapies. You need a rigorous cadence of healing right now. If you dedicate–" She interrupted herself, jutting out her bottom lip and examining Lissa's pupils. "I'm a trained face reader, so don't mind the staring. It's part of the process. Every pore tells your story."

Lissa tried not to cringe. "Um, okay."

She was promised a robust schedule that Glenda called a "pre-scription" She explained, "Your entire schedule will be on the app by the end of the day, along with step-by-step instructions. Please take time to read and study. Don't rush. I can see you struggle with pa-tience."

Lissa wondered which of her pores had betrayed her. She not-ed the easy confidence both Doreen and Glenda had, and she decided that they were proof it was possible. A small part of her even felt something like excitement when the to-do list arrived the next morn-ing. She followed the regimen Glenda had created to pass the time in a systematic way. The structure gave her peace, and she enjoyed sampling new therapies, such as a table called the vortex that would ro-tate her slowly as music attuned to specific hertz levels permeated her body. She also grew to enjoy the simple meditation room, which she had to herself every day from 10-11 a.m., after the sensory deprivation tank and before reiki.

Each of the half-dozen staff members offered a unique modality of healing, and all of them seemed to care about the residents' wellbeing. Lissa was booked morning to night with various appointments that promised to calibrate her mind, body, and spirit, and while she often thought she could be working in a factory sorting clothes, as she had in college, or bagging groceries, as she had in high school, and feel the same mild contentedness of perpetual distraction, she tried to remain open-minded. Before Trent, she'd been a seeker. But one day, while she was at work, Trent had donated her books by the Dali Lama, Starhawk, and Pema Chödrön to Half-price Books.

"We'll get a steak dinner for these," he'd said.

They got five dollars, and Lissa said nothing. Inside, she raged. She wished him dead. She'd imagined pawning all his tools for a couple bottles of wine. But that day, she only gritted her back teeth and stared at him, past him, waiting for what was next. She'd been planning to leave then. She'd been planning to leave so many times.

Able to comfortably accommodate no more than twenty residents at a time, TLC held twelve women and two men the weeks Lissa lived there, and for each person who found support, there were two who left early. For every three people who graduated, so to speak, one would return to the abuser. These were statistics that were better than those from the traditional rehabilitation centers, so Glenda and Doreen shared them freely and with pride. They liked to emphasize that those who'd been successful seemed to truly thrive, and not in ordinary ways.

There were success stories from those who stuck to their prescriptions that Lissa could read on the center's app. Famous actors and scientists alike had found their way after arriving at TLC beaten down and with nothing. Their testimonials suggested that at one time, they had as little hope as Lissa had felt with Trent.

One morning at 4 a.m., after a deep but short sleep, Lissa wandered to the common room before most residents were up and found letters of gratitude from previous residents stuffed to the brim of a decorative box on the bookshelf. She wasn't convinced she'd ever come up with a testimonial to put up on the wall or write a letter so inspiring. She wouldn't go back to Trent either, but she couldn't see anything else for her life beyond long-term mediocrity. She'd wasted too much time. What was she even supposed to do now? Find another job at a bike shop, managing one maybe? Or as a teacher? She'd probably have to sub again before she could find another full-time job, but she did love helping people. Feeling useful.

She felt this way—busy with delightful appointments but still pessimistic about what was waiting for her outside—until Annika arrived.

On the second intake Monday that September, Lissa was examining the bookshelf by the window. It'd been spitting rain all day, and many of the residents were playing cards in the living room nearby, which was adorned by garish floral-print wallpaper and banker lamps on claw-footed side tables. It was shortly after dinner, and Lissa was hoping for something untherapeutic. A good mystery or romance novel; some true escapism since there was no Netflix or HBO Max allowed. The closest she could find were Carlos Castaneda's books. She picked up *Journey to Ixtlan* and a few books on crystals and moved to sit down in one of the comfy chairs nearby when she heard the heavy front door open.

Some residents were watching cooking shows, and late '80s ballads were barely audible from Marc's headphones. One of the two men to ever be in residence at TLC, Marc didn't seem to want to leave. Five-foot-nothing and weighing at least ten pounds less than Lissa, he could bake so well that the residents had requested he host dessert night for dinner once a week, during which Marc would be bombarded with requests. It was obvious he liked the attention. His vegan cayenne brownies were so perfect that no one complained about hearing Journey and David Bowie while they ate. In fact, no one complained about much of anything until Annika arrived.

They were used to seeing residents arrive with black eyes or a broken arm, but Annika looked like something out of a horror movie when she entered the large foyer. She was greeted by both Glenda and Doreen, who seemed especially eager to greet her. Everyone stared as she walked in. She stood around Lissa's height, with a slender frame and jawline. Her face was covered in purple bruises that were only partially concealed by her thick-framed black glasses. Her tattooed arm was in a sling, and two fresh welts protruded near the crown of her head and eyebrow. When she surveyed the room, her eyes were calm, yet intense. Despite her small frame and physical state, she stood tall.

She walked up to Marc and said something under her breath that made him remove his headphones. When she was safely out of earshot, he widened his eyes. "She looks like she was attacked by an animal," Marc said, and the other residents mumbled their assessments. "I give her a 9.5," someone muttered.

"Who said that? Stop it," Amber hissed. Once a youth pastor's wife, Amber didn't find humor in the fact that residents rated each other upon entry on a scale from 1 to 10. Lissa had been a 7, or so she'd heard. Amber had been a 5. She'd tackled her husband after the third sexual misconduct charge was filed against him. In response, he beat her up pretty good, but unlike most of the residents, she was relatively safe. Her husband would be in prison for decades, and her abuse case could add a few years at least.

"Look, it's better to have a sick sense of humor than none at all," Marc said. "And don't hiss at me."

"I didn't hiss," Amber said, crossing her arms over her chest.

"You hissed," Lissa assured her, and that was the end of it. For some reason, when Lissa spoke, her words were final. At least, at TLC. That was before Annika arrived and took charge.

When Annika took Lissa's seat at the table for dinner, it was a minor annoyance. But who could admit such a thing? When she took seconds of dessert before everyone else had their single serving, Lissa decided she deserved it—eating must have been painful. Annika was an undeniable 9.5, a 10 being on the verge of death. A 9.5 deserved an extra dessert.

"So, what brings you here?" Marc asked, his chin balanced on his fist. He liked to lean in journalist-style and interview newbies.

"She tried to kill me. I tried to run. She was stronger."

"We all have similar stories, and we'll heal better together, or so the volunteer nurses tell us. They're a little woo woo."

Annika's eyes widened. "I'm a witch. I like woo woo." She dug in her large bag to retrieve a book on energy work and another on crystals. "I'm going to heal with woo woo. In fact, I'm standing here because of woo woo. I wouldn't still be in the body without it."

"Can I look at those?" Lissa asked.

Annika stared deeply into Lissa's eyes, the way an old friend would, as though trying to tease out motivation for an unexpected request. It was a moment of softness. "Of course, but I'm still reading this one." She shoved the book on energy work over and pulled the one about crystals close, as though Lissa might steal it.

Lissa liked Annika. She couldn't put her finger on it, but she somehow felt a connection with her. She invited her to yoga—begged, actually—and after some convincing, Annika agreed, though she admitted she wasn't the yoga type. The women traded notes on their lives, and though Lissa was mildly intimidated, their conversations flowed. It seemed serendipitous that they ended up being roommates, and after a quiet woman named Bee elected to leave a month ahead of schedule, there was no one in the room next to them for a few days, which gave them both permission to share their stories honestly.

They would trade notes about what they read; they'd borrow books online by the dozens, testing each other's knowledge about healing and the occult and prophecy as though they were preparing for certification. Often, they would sit in silence, reading and burning herbs. They stared out into the woods that extended beyond the drive, waiting for deer to graze or for the occasional fox to sit nearby the house and watch, stoically, as though *Waiting for Godot*. They watched from their bedroom window as a resident, a small woman with a perpetually loose ponytail and history of being sex trafficked, ducked into the back of a BMW. The woman glanced back toward the house, meeting eyes with Lissa.

"Doesn't have a chance," Annika said. "I had a dream about her last night."

"Maybe you're wrong," Lissa said.

Annika looked as though she wished what Lissa was saying could be true. "I had a dream about you, too."

"Do I have a chance?"

"You have to fight. But yeah, you have a good chance. She doesn't."

Lissa wondered if all witches were psychic. She'd always wondered about such things, but her spiritual seeking thus far had ended with simple meditations and basic yogic mindfulness. The way Annika carried herself, as though the earth and sky both lived inside of her, as though no matter what had happened to her body, she was in touch with the unbreakable within her, encouraged Lissa. Annika was the epitome of strength.

Annika's bleak prediction rang true, as would just about everything she'd say. Lissa took note of Annika's hard-edged honesty, which contrasted with her often-distant gaze.

A month or so in, Annika was doing a tarot reading for another resident for a little cash. The woman, a grandmother at fifty and suffering a broken rib from the wrath of her husband (of thirty years), was on edge, waiting for good news that Annika would not provide.

Lissa was reading by the window, trying to ignore the woman's crying. She wanted to tell Annika to take it easy on the woman and just tell her something good, even if it wasn't true. Maybe the woman could make it true if she had something to believe in. Just as she went to stand, she heard scraping.

When he wanted to intimidate her, Trent had always scraped his key—or anything sharp—against whatever surface he could find. Today, it was the brick wall that separated them. Lissa's body felt like lead, but she knew she was being paranoid. How could he possibly have found her? She crouched down to close the window and focus on her breath. Reaching to close it, she felt the window open instead and then she saw him. Her heart surged as a thick, familiar hand grabbed her throat; she glimpsed his face shrouded in a camouflage hunting net, then felt her head jerk forward. It was too late to scream or move out of the way.

"He's here," she tried to scream, but he had her breath. He's here, she screamed inside. Help.

"You sent me to prison. You really fucking sent me to prison?" he growled in her ear. No one heard her struggle against the window. When he opened it further and tried to pull her out, she felt herself separate from her body, as she had so many times when they were still together.

She was hovering somewhere outside her body when she heard the first knock on the door, then the sound of someone shoving forcefully into it. She felt the pressure release as the door burst open. She saw light.

Nana?

Pauline

Pauline **stared at the mansion** in the middle of the woods, filled with wispy women in monochrome colors with vacant eyes. Her cult radar was on high-alert, and it took every ounce of restraint to not follow her daughter into this "treatment center" and ask about methodology and credentials. She was sure there wasn't a single PhD in the place.

Lissa had always been a dreamy girl, like her father, so it wasn't a surprise she wanted to come to a place like this that promised a bit of magic to heal as though . . . Poof! No more problems. The girl's naivety had always gotten her in trouble, all the way back to when she hung out with that little kleptomaniac down the street, Ellen, who planted some stolen cherry cough drops on Lissa when the two of them got stopped by security at the grocery store after their first day of middle school.

It hadn't been a surprise that Lissa was innocent. There was no doubt. And, sadly, it hadn't been a surprise that the girl had thought there was good in Trent, who Pauline saw as tainted goods the moment they met. Lissa simply hadn't lived enough, and she'd been particularly fragile that year and resistant to therapy, per usual. Pauline blamed her entire generation for spoiling kids and coddling them to the point that they lost all their common sense, but Lissa was even worse off than most. Not only was she dreamy, but after Michael died the girl forgot who she was.

She'd floundered, diving into one obsession then the next, till she met that asshat, Trent, who eagerly gave her a shot of adrenaline, which Pauline had to admit she would've felt at Lissa's age, too. Sure, he was charming. Yes, his smile could buckle a knee or two, but his intense gaze and quick humor were all hollow charisma. Textbook. He was as unstable as he was handsome, a raging pile of testosterone— likely thanks to all the supplements and weightlifting he did.

Pauline still remembered clenching her jaw so tight that she broke a crown when Lissa sobbed and giggled on the phone like a teenager the day she announced their engagement. Trent had asked her to marry him in the middle of the city park during a surprise picnic on her lunch break from the bike shop, where she'd worked through college; she'd said yes without thinking and relayed it all tearfully to Pauline, who felt her world collapse beneath the weight of worry. Two months of dating. Eight weeks.

"Are you sure? Are you absolutely sure?" Pauline had asked, and her daughter grew silent. She refused to take Pauline's calls for a week after that. So Pauline didn't ask again. Everyone told her she was being overbearing. But love isn't always cushy and fun. Love, real love, means truth, Pauline thought. She gripped the wheel.

As anticipated, Trent had been all calculated charm and kind chitchat during the engagement, but just after the wedding he quickly showed flickers of his true self, the sociopath. His parents blamed the pandemic for his darkening moods and increased tolerance for brown liquor, but Pauline had noticed the smaller things long before: the way he cut Lissa down when she was happy, always interrupting her laughter, or shushed her when she spoke loudly. He came up with excuses for why they shouldn't go to dinners with Lissa's college friends, and he instigated the so-called lack of appreciation she was shown at work, trying to get her to quit.

"They should pay you what you're worth," he'd told Lissa when she started substitute teaching, and he ramped up his campaign when she got a full-time job.

"What teacher gets paid well when they first start?" Pauline had started, but Lissa didn't listen. She didn't understand the correlation between Trent and her anxious thoughts. The girl wasn't herself anymore. She became paranoid and nervous all the time.

"I think he's right, Mom. We can live off his salary for a while." The isolation that came with intermittent lockdowns during the pandemic only worked to magnify his controlling tendencies and her anxiety.

"Calm down," he'd bark when Lissa laughed too loud or let one of her cute snorts slip out. He'd place his large hand on her thigh as though keeping her from getting away from herself, like her joy was an embarrassment and something she should be ashamed of. It was no coincidence that Lissa's childhood anxiety had returned during that marriage, and Pauline didn't think it past Trent to share only the worst news about the virus he could find. He reinforced unhealthy habits, like staying at home every night, and shut down her unconventional spiritual beliefs, which Pauline wasn't necessarily a fan of either, but the girl had free will.

She'd tried to give the girl tools to work through her anxiety.

Helping her with cognitive behavioral techniques when they spoke on the phone, teaching her to count down when she felt the panic swell, to question her more irrational thoughts. But CBT only worked when there wasn't actually something to be paranoid about. Lissa blamed the pandemic for her anxiety. Pauline knew better.

It may or may not have been a conscious choice when Pauline had indulged in one too many martinis before her daughter's wedding and had almost driven directly into the cake display, which had tackily been a reproduction of a lawn—a homage to Trent's work as a landscaper. Reason and rationale hadn't worked, so she'd resorted to mayhem, but that didn't work either. Driving toward their outdoor ceremony and scaring the fifty-plus people standing nearby—mostly Trent's wealthy but shady family—wasn't what she felt bad about after. She felt bad about not driving a few more feet and taking that asshole out. Or, at the very least, not warning her daughter more urgently earlier, and she'd never let the girl go that easy again.

After Trent pushed Lissa to stop fulltime work and just stay on as a sub for "flexibility," she lost more of her power. Soon she became like soft clay that he could mush up into whatever shape he wanted. He continued to work, of course, helping to run his family's landscaping business—and never, as far as Pauline could tell, wearing a mask when he was out in the world during the height of the pandemic, even though he'd tell Lissa to double-mask if she so much as went grocery shopping. He'd often chastise her for not "giving him kids yet," and when Lissa called Pauline to say, shakily, maybe she'd made a mistake, Pauline hadn't gotten there early enough to save her daughter from his brutality.

"Fucker!" Pauline said, both to herself and him, squeezing the steering wheel till her knuckles went white. She caught her image in the rearview and adjusted her graying bangs, which were getting long. "Never. Never will you touch my daughter again, Trent. I will kill you."

Pauline started the engine upon noticing a set of gray eyes on her. The woman who had greeted Lissa looked as though she'd been transported from Woodstock. The woman lifted her hand in a gentle wave, and Pauline rolled her eyes. She saluted before turning and beginning the drive home. Trying not to clench her jaw, she spoke to herself the way she often recommended clients do. *"I am not these emotions. I am here. Driving. Focusing on the road in front of me. I am breathing. It is Tuesday. I smell the dampness in the air. I am alert, and I am here. My daughter is safe. I am not in the past."*

But the mention of the past shifted Pauline's thoughts again, back to what her daughter had lost. Who they had both lost. Michael. He'd been a psychologist, like her, who had specialized in cognitive behavioral therapy and often lectured at various universities toward the end of his career, as he wanted to focus more on research. He was persistent and tidy and had washboard abs into his forties. And when he got into cycling, he had even started waxing his legs, which Pauline had resisted at first, then learned to enjoy.

She chuckled, trying to ignore the deer skull she glimpsed by a firepit on her way off the grounds. By his last years on the planet, Michael was entering at least half a dozen biathlons a year and teaching qigong on Sundays. A bit of a magical thinker himself, he was also a brilliant scientific mind, and he had a way of connecting with Lissa when she was young that Pauline could never replicate. If only he'd been around to warn her daughter away from Trent. Lissa would've listened to him without question, Pauline was sure.

She stopped the car on the gravel road, where there was a creaky gate that opened inwards to let her out. She glanced back at the house, catching sight of a few wild sunflowers that swayed in the humid breeze, then thought of Michael again, the familiar ache of his absence returning. She didn't believe in such things, but perhaps just this once she'd imagine he was looking out for his daughter. Maybe he was looking out for both of them.

Pauline smiled at the thought, recalling how Michael always greeted her with sunflowers for her birthday, adding a flower each year they were together. They'd spent weekends on roads like these, hiking and taking long rides in the Cuyahoga Valley National Park, passing horses along the Ohio and Erie Canal. As kind as he was, he cursed more than anyone she'd ever met, and had a dry humor. Always willing to poke fun at himself, he'd often channel Oscar Wilde when he had a second helping of rigatoni to carb-load after a race, declaring, "I can resist anything except pasta … and most other things I like."

She eased the car forward, but the gate had given up on her and was beginning to close again. She backed up the car and lurched forward once more, this time noticing a car barreling toward the gate on the other side. As the gate creaked open again, the two cars could barely pass each other, and the girl in the other car, all bruises and black clothes, yelled something inaudible at Pauline.

"I am driving. I am calm. I am empathetic," Pauline said, closing

her eyes and taking a breath. She practiced a compassion exercise she often gave to clients, glancing back at the beat-up Jeep the woman was driving and saying, *"I wish you peace. I wish you love. I wish you to live with ease."* Then she barreled forward herself, making her way onto a busier road without looking. A truck driver leaned on the horn for at least twenty seconds, but Pauline didn't care. She glanced into the rear-view and squinted her eyes, thick with mascara top and bottom, till she could make out the driver's face. Once she saw it, she thought about the compassion exercise but instead lifted her middle finger at him and hit the gas again.

All those years ago now, Michael had invited Pauline to join him on a bike ride, but she hadn't felt up to it. She'd ignored the twinge of regret she felt when he left, then tried to rationalize his lateness by dinnertime. But after two hours of calling him with no answer and trying to file a missing person report, which she couldn't because he hadn't been gone long enough, she'd begun to search the familiar routes. The phone call from the police a few hours later after a young man had found him while jogging, nearly broke Pauline in half. Michael had died suddenly of a heart attack as he was biking alone.

Over the last few years, she'd tried to comfort herself by thinking about how torturous living through the pandemic of the 20s would've been for her husband, an extrovert who always needed to be on the move, who was always fueled by frenetic energy, but she knew better.

Had he been around, everything would've been better. They might've lived with ease.

Annika

When **Annika arrived at The Lavender Center,** everything in her body was pulsing. Her psychic abilities were amplified, as they often were during times of transition, which was agitating. Even more so than the obvious pain from her swollen, broken face.

The constant chatter of others' thoughts made her teeth itch as she evaluated the room of people staring at her. Desperation and judgment emanated from the residents. All but one: a slight woman, with thick dark hair and high cheekbones. The woman's nose looked too thin to breathe through, and this might've been true—her breath was shallow enough that her chest barely moved. But there was something else about her. Something different.

She wore a nametag, as they all did. Lissa. There was no flower, star, or moonbeam drawn next to this woman's name like other residents who seemed to be trying to convince themselves of something. Annika respected this. We'll be friends, she thought as she offered the woman a slight nod.

Annika could hear everyone's thoughts, but not all at once. Usually, the most extreme emotions resonated the loudest, and the rest were just background noise. She heard the calculations one resident was making above the rest.

"She looks terrifying. An 8 or 8.5. Maybe it was self-defense," the stocky woman in yoga pants thought. This "rating" system on the abuser beat-down scale, and the inappropriate stories many of the residents attached to Annika's appearance rolled from one prefrontal cortex to another. The groupthink was disgusting. Never one to play the victim, Annika had to change this narrative fast. Her father had taught her this. Take control of the territory and the vibe. It wouldn't take long.

"You should see the other guy," she told the woman in yoga pants, who smiled. Annika did not.

The truth was that, though Annika could've easily stopped her ex mid-attack and avoided this whole scenario, she hadn't. And she hadn't because a small part of her was hoping the rage would success-fully take her out. She was tired of her magic and of being unable to turn off the constant bombardment of chatter in her head.

This affliction was a gift from her mentor, Inga, who seemed to think there should be no limits on a person's magic, and had encour-aged Annika, when she was still quite young, to amplify her skills. Af-ter attending only three celebrations as a self-declared sorceress, Inga pulled the girl close and whispered that she recognized her gift. But after working with Inga for a year, this gift turned into a burden she couldn't find a way to release.

To read a person's thoughts was torture because, while any individual's thoughts are rough, hearing the neuroses of others like a constant thrum in the back of her mind made Annika resentful. Whether she wanted to or not, she heard too much. She could look down the street and see the impending accident as someone thought to check their email in light traffic.

She once heard the inner monologue of a truck driver willing-ly swerving into heavy traffic because of his own sadness, without any concern about who he'd take down with him. Annika was too far away to warn anyone. She heard him as he consciously decided to swerve at an angle that would give him his peace, to hell with any casualties. Annika heard the hatred, greed, lust, and competition that lived behind seemingly innocuous smiles. She heard the navel-gazing personaliza-tion of every news story and every public loss.

The beating she had endured had been a version of this, An-nika supposed. The fight itself had arrived almost as though it was a third party, after Annika told her girlfriend, now ex, what her drinking would lead to if she didn't stop. Kat's conscious unraveling took a shadowy appearance as it descended on Annika, body checking her after knocking her to the ground. "I'll just have two more. I'll put one in the freezer, so it'll be ready. Annika is probably going to give me shit. I'm sick of her acting like my mother," Kat had said an hour ago, too drunk to realize Annika could hear her from the bathroom.

With Annika outweighed and staring up at her enraged lover, she mustered the words, "I want to take a break."

"This isn't *Friends*. You can't say that to me." Kat was already four beers in, so the timing was off, but somehow what began as a simple argument spiraled out of hand, and instead of getting up, Kat sat on Annika and stared down at her as though she were prey. When Annika spit, she knew what would come next. She was egging it on, and sure, she'd lost the fistfight, but she hadn't lost the war. She played on every thought, poking and provoking, and each time Kat would seem to retreat, there was another soft spot.

"What? You think leaving bruises on me will keep me around? You're just showing how much like your family you are," she growled. Kat lunged toward her again.

Annika had never practiced vengeful magic before, and she'd been momentarily tempted with Kat. But it wasn't necessary. The future in this case was easy to predict. When she looked at Kat, she saw the image of energy spiraling in the wrong direction, unraveling her. Annika left her ex-fiancé's apartment battered, but the life of the woman she left behind would soon be in ruins. A painfully slow drowning. An addiction that wouldn't allow her to surface again.

"Poor woman," another resident, a scrawny man whose jaw was moving as though he was constantly grinding his teeth, thought.

Annika marched up to him, appreciating the sound of Bowie threading through his headphones. "Don't pity me," she said into his ear. "I think you should hold your judgment. I also think you should lower the volume on your device. You hear the birdsong and waves and shit this place plays? They do it for a reason. Bowie's great, but people need to heal. Lower the volume. Keep him to yourself while you're in here." She looked around the room, relishing the silence of thought, and tracked only one bit of internal monologue.

"Bad ass. Wish I had that kind of power," the slight woman with the thick dark hair thought.

Annika walked up to her next, ignoring the way she recoiled at the fast approach. "Can you show me around?"

"Um, sure. I'm new myself, but I'll do my best. This place is interesting. Let's walk." The woman, who introduced herself as Lissa, had a scar that traced her neck across external carotid arteries. Someone had wanted to kill this woman genuinely and intentionally, and Annika wanted to know why. One of the limitations of Annika's abilities was tapping the past. She couldn't see anything beyond what people were thinking at the moment. She had to come to her own conclusions about what had led people to their current states, which she knew could be dangerous; after all, context was everything, and it was easy to be unfair to people based on a single thought or two.

At TLC, Annika resolved to be more diligent and thoughtful, especially when she practiced magic. Otherwise, she could be short-sighted. At the time of her arrival, she couldn't imagine herself someone's mentor, but she knew there was something pulling her toward Lissa and pulling her toward transition.

"Do you like yoga?" Lissa asked, and Annika could hear her internal hope.

"I'll try it out. I'm more of a runner," she said.

"Oh, good. I love it, but only a few people show up, and I'm worried they'll cancel it. Please come, at least once."

"You worry too much," Annika said.

Lissa stopped and stared. "Is it that obvious? My worry?"

"I'm intuitive," Annika said, peeking in a room that held a floatation tank, which was lit up in purple. A shower with a waterfall showerhead stood behind it. "Sensory deprivation? Impressive. No wonder this place is expensive."

"I don't know how I'm going to repay my credit cards," Lissa confided. "I was an out-of-work teacher. This place is breaking me financially."

"Feel ya. I have a bit of money stuffed away that I had been planning to use to start a business when the government incentives were offered, but here we are instead" Annika, for all her suffering, didn't know what it was to be truly broke. Magic had afforded her pain, but it also gave her power. She had over eighty thousand in her account, which she'd inherited from a grandmother she adored. Her parents had died in a house fire four years earlier, which made the loss hit her all the harder. She used to call her grandmother Grandma Glam because she was always so well put together and simply got used to vacations in Hawaii or family cruises when she was younger.

"One day, all this bullshit will be behind us. I just wish I could see it," Lissa said. "You know, I wanted to start a nonprofit a long time ago. Something about education, tutoring. I never thought it through."

"I see it. Why a nonprofit?"

"To help people, I guess. To give something back and fill the gaps in education I saw. The disparity in this country exists because of the disparity in access to education."

Annika stared at Lissa for a long time, assessing what she couldn't hear or sense. Lissa had a vibe she'd been drawn to, but was she trustworthy? People who have been through trauma could adopt odd habits to survive, and some of them could be destructive. Most abusers were trauma survivors, after all. Case in point, Kat. Taking a chance, Annika reached for Lissa's hand. "You know I'm a witch, right?"

Lissa laughed. "Wiccan?"

"Witch. It's my practice, not my religion, but it's also serious. What do you think when I say that?" she asked, listening to her new friend's thoughts.

I want to learn, Lissa thought. "It's interesting," she said out loud.

"I'll teach you," Annika offered. The only way out of a problem is to dig in, her father used to say. She knew that the same intuition that tortured her was also what she needed to tap into to move forward, to start fresh. The time for Inga's kind of magic was over; it was her time to learn through teaching.

Annika had plans of hiving—starting her own coven—after the breakup, and after witnessing some odd, possibly outright sick behaviors from her teacher-turned-guru. Inga charged people between a couple hundred and a thousand dollars for a spell. For years, Annika had practiced magic with a small group of women and men in her hometown, but Inga was their High Priestess, who also happened to be Kat's aunt.

The family's extreme views seemed to be magnified lately, and Annika could only hope that her beat-down made her appear enough of a victim that they would leave her alone. Though Annika wasn't too fearful of any recourse for leaving Kat, she had seen them hurt people before. A neighborhood woman who had refused to serve Inga at a diner one day, had suddenly ended up with Ebola. This had been Annika's first clue that she might want to find a different group.
True magic, to Annika, wasn't ever about revenge. An autodidact at heart, she'd studied enough to know that the most powerful magic came from a place of personal connection, not external destruction. To manipulate another person's energy was to feed it, in one way or another.

She watched Lissa's face each night as she explained the basics to her, little by little, and felt proud of herself. An odd feeling. This is true magic though: spinning the web out of thin air and making the world a better place. She felt that her bond with Lissa would be a good start. They were both in Geodon, Ohio, both from around Akron, though they'd never run into each other. Lissa was green for a coven, but she seemed committed.

Over the next few months, as Annika began to teach her the basics: sigils, scrying, navigating the astral plane, remote viewing, and candle magic, Lissa showed enormous potential and enthusiasm. It seemed that the magic was giving her agency, just as it had for Annika. Annika had been excited to give her friend a gift: her first book of shadows. One night, after the dinner they were all "strongly encouraged" to join with the other residents, she told Lissa to wait and scrounged around looking for something to wrap the notebook in.

"Can I help you, dear?" Glenda said, materializing with no thought in her head, which always creeped Annika out. She was dressed in a cowl neck tan shirt and wide-legged white pants.

"Yes. I'm looking for something to wrap this in. I want to give Lissa a gift."

"Oh! Is it her birthday? I thought I was on top of all the birthdays around here."

"No, just a gift from a friend. She likes to write."

Glenda clapped her hands. "How nice! You know, Annika, I had some concerns about you. You seem overcome by your rage at times."

"I get that way, yeah."

"Have you tried the meditation room? Not once, but daily? I think twenty minutes a day for a full month would do wonders."

Annika didn't want to tell this woman that she already meditated for an hour every morning, connecting to goddess energy and mother earth. She didn't want to tell her that she'd already practiced or tried everything this place offered many times over. Nothing felt new. The absence of audible thoughts made Annika wonder if Glenda had a shield up.

"I know I can be a little . . . abrasive, but I'm working through it. I lost the love of my life to fucking beer, and I tried to absorb her pain. I tried to take it from her, and maybe I actually did."

"Do you believe that? That you absorbed her pain? And do you feel like your efforts here are helping?"

"I am putting in the effort. Believe me."

"And nothing's working. Nothing's helping."

"Nothing's new. It all feels hollow."

Glenda put a slender hand on Annika's back, and Annika tried not to flinch. Her soft, low voice was like a melody. "You're doing well, all things considered. There's no need to try to read my thoughts. I'm focused on you. And I understand the burden you carry—you shouldn't have to. Perhaps a different kind of connection will be more helpful." Before Annika could respond, Glenda pulled out a shiny piece of silver paper. "This should do you. A blocking spell. It's temporary but will help when you feel overwhelmed. Tomorrow is the new moon. I will be here if you're interested."

Annika took the paper, which had a simple candle spell on it and a business-card-sized map that showed the way to a clearing in the woods. "I'll be there tomorrow. What about—?"

"Lissa may come, but only if you think she's ready. I'll leave that up to you."

Annika rushed to retrieve Lissa, genuinely excited to implement the candle spell she'd received, but when she arrived at the door, it was jammed. She knocked and called out, but no one answered. She could hear something heavy drop and a muffled sound—a struggle.

Help, Lissa thought. Her thoughts screamed, panicked.

Annika kicked at the door. The muffled sound stopped and a new sound began, something like a garbage disposal. Annika called for someone to find Glenda, trying to tune into Lissa's thoughts, but got only occasional flickers. She feared her new friend might fade completely.

Residents emerged from their rooms and stood in the hallways, glancing around nervously as Annika continued to ram herself into the door. Finally, she stood back and closed her eyes. Glenda arrived with a key, and the residents rushed in to find Lissa on the floor by the window, gasping for breath. A shadowy figure at the window turned and ran into the woods.

Oh, no worries. He's not going anywhere, Glenda thought. Annika looked up toward her new mentor, who was comforting Lissa and nodded. The man running away from the window and toward the street tripped over something and fell hard. He was dressed in camouflage, and Annika stood at the window, holding him to the ground with her gaze. He would be in prison or worse in no time.

She looked to Glenda as she kneeled next to her new friend, and the two of them shared a single thought: This is how new beginnings truly started. Despite the fact that they were in the middle of nowhere, the police arrived promptly and arrested Trent, Lissa's husband, and medics cleared Lissa. He hadn't done any major damage aside from some new bruising, but the impact of his presence on her equilibrium and sense of security could only be remedied by magic. She was able to stay at TLC, and when asked if there was anyone they should call, she begged Glenda and Doreen not to tell her mother everything—only that he'd shown up and been arrested.

"I'll fill her in on the details later," she promised them, sitting on Annika's bed.

"Like you can lie to a witch," Annika said. "I know you're shaken up, but you're safe now." She held her new friend close, and the two rocked like children. It was here with Lissa's head on Annika's chest, when she felt something she hadn't in years. Her cheeks began to swell more than they already were and a few fresh tears escaped from her makeup-darkened eyes. She wiped away the black lines. She stayed with Lissa, doing everything she could to absorb her friend's pain.

Doreen and Glenda led Annika to the firepit as the sun began to set.

"We want to settle into the energy of the night before we begin our work. Tonight is about healing, for our friend Lissa and us all. Let's take some time to connect to the healing pulse of the earth before we begin," Glenda said.

The three women stared into the flames, wordless, searching for the center. It was a cool evening, and Annika had been welcomed without the bother of formality. She was surprised no one else joined them and wondered if this was some sort of test but immediately detracted from the thought when Glenda looked up.

It was more than a little disconcerting to know she wasn't the only one who could hear thoughts, but Annika trusted these women. She trusted them in a way she hadn't trusted Inga or most anyone before. She could see that they were doing the work they were meant to do. And as she recentered herself, she heard a message loud and clear, perhaps from Doreen or Glenda, perhaps from her own mind. She would have to do the same.

When the sky darkened to indigo and the flame began to reduce, Annika broke the silence. "I'm on to you ladies," she said. "This is therapy for me, too."

"Indulge us," Doreen said. "Help us feed the fire, there!" She pointed toward a small clearing with a firepit. Glenda walked behind them; her footfall barely audible, and the three women began to collect a few dry branches and brush.

"The problem with life is the problem with love," Annika explained. "It hurts. People glorify the hurt, songs romanticize it, but pain is pain is pain. Love is trust, and trust is the most vulnerable of human emotions and, unlike animals, we humans are shit at moving on with our lives when we're disappointed. We try the slot machine again, even if we don't have any money left."

The trees outside TLC clung tight to their vivid orange and

deep red leaves. As they turned back to the fire, Doreen asked, "What if love just is, and we can't control it?"

Doreen reminded Annika vaguely of her mother—a gentle but strong woman who specialized in international law and was almost never home. Annika's father had raised her well, but he never understood how to talk to her. He always seemed so intent on toughening her up so she could face the world that he forgot to show tenderness. She saw her father then, dapper in his suit, and her mother, swirling around in a knee-length gold gown that shimmered. They would go to parties when her mother was home and leave her at a neighbor's house, but this was the last one. She loved her parents and remembered trusting that they knew better than to stay too late at a party. She'd trusted that they'd always come home, until they didn't.

"Honey," Glenda said, reaching out. "You can love again. You already do."

Annika glanced over at a shallow area where a toad was croaking, perhaps to announce the sunset or tell them to look out toward the lavender sky. *If only I could hear the thoughts of animals instead of people.*

"I know I'm being dramatic, but for all my fancy insights, I can't pick the people I love for shit. And love sucks."

"Friendship is love, and you're finding that here," Glenda said, shaking her head knowingly. "And you might be able to tune into a few animals. Things are forever in flux, even our gifts."

Annika took an audible breath and tried not to show her annoyance that Glenda had read her digressive thought. Glancing toward the two women, she allowed a soft smile to cross her face. She didn't always have to be hard like her father. "I appreciate you both. Thank you for not patronizing me."

"Never," they both said.

"I have a lot of respect for what you do here, your magic as a healing modality, etc…., but I'm just not that soft and fluffy. I loved my ex-girlfriend. She practiced the craft, but she turned out to be a crazy drunk. My mentor turned me into this … person who can't function because I can hear everyone's thoughts. It seems like everything I love ends up hurting me."

"Not everything. A lot of people who are gifted turn to distractions, but you can move beyond that," Doreen said. A buck stared at them from behind a pine, his eyes unmoving, and Annika tried to tune into his mind. She imagined he was thinking these three odd creatures looked innocent enough, but he had better watch them anyway. He had a family to protect.

When she noticed Glenda staring at her, she said, "Okay, so I'm being dramatic again. But love hurts, and it's hard to sign up for things that hurt."

"You knew that. You knew all of that when you met everyone you ever loved," Glenda said. "With time you'll find that not everything has to hurt. Maybe at times, but it doesn't have to end with hurt. We can change our stories. You have that power more than most."

"So what do I change it to?" She could hear the deer rustling behind them, rushing back into the depth of the woods.

"You see that tree? Come. Follow us," Glenda said.

The women walked into the forest, until the path narrowed toward a mossy bed at the base of the widest tree Annika had ever seen. "Beautiful," she said, glancing up as she walked around it, palm to bark.

"This is the mother tree—the oldest tree in the forest. She's lived through so many different conditions that she is adaptable, knowledgeable. She's able to nourish the soil and send messages that reach the roots of younger trees."

"The other trees do not have to be near her to be nurtured by her. The entire forest relies on her wisdom. It spans beyond space and time. Love is like that. Maternal love is especially like that. Your love for others is like that, too. They might not be able to appreciate it, but if your offering was genuine, know that it was a gift."

"A gift that hurt. I was lonely and fascinated. I let myself fall in love, trust people," Annika admitted. "I never thought I'd find someone like me, you know, who knew how to use the affliction for good." She tapped her temple, trying to ignore Doreen's soft-eyed sympathy.

Glenda smiled. "We're rarely gifted and not also cursed, my dear. There are polarities to life. I'll teach you, over time. But for now, you need to embrace your role. You are in a position to support others, and we all need to ensure our girl is safe. Before we cast the circle, I need you to be honest with me. Do you think Lissa's ready?"

No, Annika thought. She figured Glenda must've heard the thought, but nonetheless she said, "Yes. Let's bring her in."

"I was hoping you'd say that," Doreen said. She clapped her hands, and Doreen floated off to retrieve Lissa as Annika and Glenda moved back toward the firepit. Annika started the fire.

"You're good at that," Glenda said.

"I was told I have a lot of fire. Aries. Leo rising."

"You know, with fire we can get away from our true intentions sometimes. A student of the craft must ask to be mentored with grace and patience. I worry about your ability to be patient." Before Annika had the chance to respond, Glenda stood, lifting her palms open to the sky and hugging her elbows to her ribs. As she glanced directly up toward the darkening sky, Annika noticed the trees around them going still, their leaves turned up.

Annika said, "Lissa's desire is strong, but her . . . spirit . . ."

"It's faded. She's not fully alive. Yet. But I'm not worried about Lissa's spirit. I'm not worried about her. We'll bring her back," Glenda said. As she lowered her hands, wispy rain drops began to fall. "Let's close our eyes."

"Shouldn't we go inside? The clouds are getting dark—or did you make it rain?" Annika said with a small laugh that went ignored.

The two sat in silence, feeling the feather-like rain fall. They sat perfectly still until the slight crunching of stones on the path signaled them to open their eyes and greet the others.

Lissa wandered out after Doreen looking slightly bewildered, and the four women sat in silence. Glenda rubbed her hands together as Doreen poured thick yellow liquid in a chalice next to each of them. Lissa took small sips of the mead nearest her, not realizing that it was for later, and looked around every few seconds, as though Trent might appear from behind a tree. *It's okay, you're safe*, Annika thought. She wished her friend would hear. Lissa looked around nervously, trying to appear as still and at ease as the rest of them.

"I'd like you to call the directions for our circle today, Annika," Doreen said. "Our ask of the goddess will be to offer protection for you and a repellant against those who are unfit to walk our grounds. We are securing our boundaries so that we have space for all who live here to heal."

When Lissa stood, she glanced around at the four simple foldout chairs circling the fire. Glenda, Annika, Doreen and Lissa each stood in front of one. Glenda raised her voice and howled toward the stars, which made Lissa take a quick step back. Annika gave her an assuring glance, wishing for once that she could share her magic as she repeated the thought that Lissa was safe and this would help. The ritual would make her strong, remind her of the support that exists all around.

"We welcome Lissa into our circle tonight as a guest," Glenda started, closing her eyes as she intoned. "Lissa, we welcome you without expectation. You may participate to your comfort level and leave at any time. We welcome Annika to our circle to call on the energies of the four directions. We know you are both pure of heart, and today we will cast a spell of protection for you. Today, we will become one, and travel to the depths to reconnect with our strength."

"Th-thank you," Lissa said as she glanced down at the mead again.

Annika stepped forward, and the two older women turned to face north. Their hands were facing forward in a pose of receptivity. She gestured for Lissa to do the same and called on the voice that lived deep within her. "To the north, we send thanks to Mother Earth, remembering she who nourishes and supports us, holding us here and grounding our energy as we journey together." Then she turned to the east. "To the winds that give us breath, we welcome vitality and the energy to do what we are meant to do. We thank you and welcome in your lifeforce." Annika turned toward the mansion, deepening her voice. "The fiery will we all keep inside gives us strength to move forward, the reminder that we deserve to thrive during our time on this planet so we may lift each other up." On the final turn, she lifted her voice higher. "And please come into us, the flowing nature of water that allows us to adapt to the constant that is change, that is this existence, feeling the seas around and inside us now as we bend and never break."

Glenda stepped forward, nodding to Annika with a maternal smile. "I call upon the goddess. We invite in our guides to join our circle, and the goddess, Hecate, who symbolizes this crossroads," she began. As she led the women to sit and meditate, they journeyed to the goddess. They welcomed her into their hearts, reconnecting and serving.

Annika felt the call in that moment to dedicate herself fully to the craft. She'd been practicing for years, but only on the periphery after getting her first degree, which essentially meant she was curious. She hadn't been through the rigor of a second degree, nor the outright terror of facing the shadow side that came with total commitment. In that moment, however, she realized she was ready. The goddess was alive inside her; she felt the steadiness of the ground. It was a connected feeling but not settled, exactly. Everything was about to change.

After closing out the circle, the mead was passed around ceremoniously, along with a small piece of cake, which each woman took a bite of. Annika looked at Lissa, who seemed to be soaking in the experience with curious disbelief.

The women sat and stared at the fire, imagining the safety and security that would allow them to connect to something deeper. It was here that Annika realized she was being called to heal as well. She got a glimpse of crystals lining the walls of a shop and a series of offerings. And Lissa, who stood behind the counter, would be her partner. She glanced over at her new friend, a person she barely knew, wishing briefly that she could see a future in which they were something more, but the trajectory seemed all business. And it wasn't bad.

"We don't have to worry about him anymore," Glenda said. "He will be locked away for some time, and we're here if you need us." Lissa appeared fully convinced, and the shadow of anxiety that followed her seemed to lift.

"That was—" She didn't seem to have the words, not even in her own mind. The soft rain had ceased, and now only a gentle wind nudged the fire. Each element was with them, inside them, and once the ceremony was over and they began to walk back to their room, Annika nudged Lissa.

"We have to talk," she said. "I'm not sure what your plans are after this place, but I think we should discuss."

Finally, hope, Annika heard Lissa think. "I agree," Lissa said, sticking out her hand. They shook, business-like, then they embraced.

Not long after that day, the two women became inseparable. They bonded over an ability to hear what they sometimes didn't want to— for Lissa, it was the dead, a gift that intrigued Annika. Her friend confided that she used to hear her great-grandmother and occasionally heard others whose relatives were sticking around them.

"Can you turn it on and off?" Annika asked, leaning in after lunch one day.

"It's not often. It was more when I was a kid. I didn't hear anything when I was with Trent, but it started to come back at the hospital. I honestly kind of wish I heard them more often."

"It's a practice, like anything, but be careful what you wish for. I hear thoughts of the living, even when I don't want to, and believe me, I wish it happened less often."

Can she hear my thoughts now? Lissa wondered.

"Yes."

Holy shit!

If they weren't meeting in the dining hall, the two new friends were always planning On their own. They hatched an idea to launch a small business in an area near a bookshop not far from where Lissa lived. Annika was a half hour away, but that would be fine. They called around to inquire about rates and as they neared time to leave the LC, they even went to visit the space that asked for reasonable rent that would make the perfect space for a small shop.

Inside an office complex, the retail space had a window facing the main street and one at the side, where a shop could display its wares. They both peered in, envisioning the metaphysical store with an emphasis on health and healing that they'd constructed over conversations. They'd offer services. Nothing as extreme as TLC, but nourishing products and tarot readings. Something to bring back a person's spirit once it's been broken or help them to connect with the spirits that surround them.

As Annika walked around to the side of the building to peer through the other window that looked out on a patch of trees, she could see the two of them inside, selling crystals and offering the sort of gentle wisdom they'd received at TLC. She also saw them arguing, but this didn't dissuade her. This was business.

"Let's call it The Sprit House, TSH for short because acronyms are best for signs," Lissa called.

"TSH has a ring to it," Annika said, sounding it out phonetically again and again between her teeth like a whisper that would call something into existence.

"I just wish we had the funds. I love talking about this, but the rent in this area is getting up there," Lissa said, and Annika could hear her continued thoughts about money. Lissa's social circle was miniscule and basically just included her mother, who had money but wouldn't approve. Lissa was envisioning her mother's voice in a high octave as she dismissed the idea of investing. *My daughter is no snake oil salesperson. Did I ever tell you about the man who got rich selling tomato seeds just by claiming they cured all that ails you? I raised you with more integrity than that.*

"I have money," Annika said loudly, trying to interrupt Lissa's thoughts. "My parents left me quite a lot. I just . . . hadn't known what to do with it till now. I can at least get us started, get some inventory."

"Are you sure? You barely know me," Lissa said.

Trust. They both thought it.

Annika didn't waver. "Let's do it. I'll help you strengthen your powers. We're going to help people. Together."

Their enthusiasm then had been genuine, and their relationship seemingly unbreakable. They pledged their reliability to each other and toasted cinnamon-laced mead to the newly formed LLC, ensuring their investment with magic by placing an image of building owner, Julianne O'Malley, in a bowl of sugar and reciting a chant to get a deal on their rent.

"I don't know about all of the things you sell, but there's something about you two I like. So long as you do good business and pay your rent, we'll get along," Julianne told Annika when they'd first signed the lease with two months' deposit.

They quickly made strategic partnerships with a few local artisans so there was less to import, and customers seemed genuinely curious about their offerings from day one. At the time, it seemed anything that wasn't mainstream was destined for success, and if Annika was anything, it was the antithesis to mainstream. This was trust. This was love in action. But a part of her knew the hurt would soon come.

The Spirit House

Everything was in flux, and a part of Lissa wished she could go back in time. She wanted to be at The Lavender Center again, cocooned in the care of Doreen and Glenda, still under the tutelage of Annika, rather than in business with her, if only to take some pressure off. Business was tough, and Lissa blamed herself—she was constantly distracted by what she knew, in her marrow, would soon come.

She took a breath and looked around. Annika was on a house call, a party in which she was to offer five Tarot readings for the bridesmaids. It was a good gig and one Lissa had hoped to help with, but someone needed to mind the shop. Sales had been steady at first, but things seemed to be slowing this month, and she was staying late most days.

While the weather had become more erratic and pollution now caused "mask days" in the states, as it did in most of the world, the good news had been the collective push toward wellness in all forms. It seemed many people were becoming more open-minded out of necessity, and Lissa was proud to share the tools that had helped her so profoundly.

She often delighted in wandering nearby neighborhoods and passing out business cards to other local businesses, looking for partnerships and bartering to find new opportunities. Her background as an educator came in handy as she offered classes on crystals and energy healing, and she was constantly studying. But there was also the other side of things: her own magic seemed somewhat beyond her control and so she often grew self-conscious when practicing and instead focused on the practical things. Business.

She and Annika had joined the Chamber of Commerce and attended networking events, where people would pretend not to be interested in such "out there" services, then slyly approach her in the parking lot and ask whether she did tarot readings or if she could help them contact their deceased grandparents.

"What are the akashic records, exactly?" the mayor had whispered after a community lunch last year.

"Do you take Saturday appointments?" a real estate agent had asked at a local tomato festival, only to slink into the shop a few days later, becoming a proud regular for a time, buying crystals and mini goddess sculptures for her friends. Back then, Lissa and Annika had received thank-you cards and homemade cookies left at the front door, instead of cryptic overdue notices.

Then came the tech industry's answer to wellness. It began with RoboHealth apps, but when the RoboHealth Assistant was unveiled, other wellness offerings began to suffer. At first, these developments seemed complementary. The technology was finally sophisticated enough to accomplish what Elizabeth Holmes had promised so many years prior. First, it could take a person's vitals and bloodwork at home and offer early warnings against terminal disease. Then, it went further, assessing symptoms in a relatively reliable way, to monitoring hormone fluctuations, even recommending complex eating and supplement regimens, along with plant medicines customized to the individual's needs.

The news occasionally highlighted stories about people who used the app irresponsibly to get prescriptions or combinations of supplements that allowed them to get high, but overall the public response had been one of pure adoration and gratitude. Still shell-shocked from the pandemic, the technology promised to alleviate the fear of another fast-spreading virus through real-time reporting. People who used it were contributing to collective health, the ads said, and insurance companies began offering discounts for owners of the technology.

Even Lissa had been enamored by wellness technology because it had been a vision of her father's. Her Assistant was a square box with a koala painted on the side, and it would sit by her bed acting as both alarm clock and doctor's assistant. The collapsible machine that accompanied the robot was easy to use and would offer comedic distractions as you placed your arm in the sleeve every six months for a blood sample. It even prepared prepaid mailing stickers. The Robo-Health Assistant would set appointments and alert you when stress monitors were activated, offering exercises to kick your parasympathetic nervous system into gear again. But Lissa didn't like how robotic she felt when she followed the regimen, and she didn't like how on bad days, it'd often recommend she begin an anti-anxiety medication.

After two months, when the app started telling her more insistently that she needed to try ayahuasca to deal with the intermittent anxiety that arrived when she saw Trent would soon be up for bail, she threw out her device and told her mother to do the same. When she tried to remove the app, it wouldn't disappear.

"I can't remove it, honey. I recommend it to clients now," Pauline had said. "Don't worry about your business. It's just temporary."

Lissa dusted the glass that held various gems twisted into jewelry with copper wire. Twenty more minutes passed before the gong sounded, signaling a customer. Twisting her hair into a haphazard bun with the rubber band, Lissa assumed her widest smile. She grabbed a fistful of selenite for protection and stood near her purse.

A woman in an animal print dress approached her with curious eyes. The woman looked around, like everyone did their first time, taking in the multisensory experience, and Lissa smiled. "Welcome to The Spirit House."

"Good afternoon. It smells like a warm hug in here."

"Clary sage. Can I help you find anything?"

"Crystals."

"Of course! Here, in case you'd like to mix and match. I like to hold each one and close my eyes, let the crystal speak to me. I'll give you time. Let me know if you have any questions." Lissa handed the woman a small velvet baggie with a pull-tie as she concentrated on the polygons and diamond shapes of the dress in front of her. Snakeskin!

"I need something for protection. Or … purging," the woman said. "I've been going through a tough time lately."

Lissa closed her eyes, directing her mind to the ocean, the waves. She considered the woman closely and noticed a trace of vulnerability, masked as annoyance. She needed help. The woman appeared stuck between two worlds, and this usually meant the past and present, though at rare times it could mean the present and future. Lissa knew this look well because she saw it in her own face most mornings when she was with Trent.

Plucking four stones from the display case, Lissa lined them up meticulously. Moving slowly was a sign of confidence and knowing that she'd amassed over these last years, she also made a point to show care and respect for the customer. She'd learned to trust herself when she was serving others, to honor their energy, but she'd never felt so out of focus and weak. "Energy must be coddled," Annika once told her, so she closed her eyes a long second, then spoke.

"The rose quartz is all about harmony. It is the stone of restoration." Lissa paused. "The moonstone is for balancing our masculine and feminine energies and magnifying experience, and the hematite grounds you and clarifies your thoughts. I would keep these two near each other."

A young man wandered around the back entrance of the building and blew plumes of smoke into the forest. He appeared faint, with a slight blue cast to his skin. She was seeing a spirit. She repeated what Annika had taught her. "The amethyst heals and raises the vibrational frequencies around you. It will help with protection. I recommend lining them up somewhere you will see them regularly and grazing your finger over them each morning and evening to remind yourself that they are there." Lissa gestured to the shop's crystal wall of protection on the windowsill.

"I don't have to carry them with me?" the woman asked.

"You can if you need support during the day. I always have stones in my pocket."

"I might do the same. But I really like jewelry." She held up her hands to show off a bundle of bracelets and rings adorning each arm. "You all do custom jewelry, right?"

"Yes, we do. That's a lovely way to keep them close. We have a guy, Raven, who can wrap the stones. He comes in on weekends, usually."

"I have to deal with this soon. I mean, I need to do something now. Can I buy one and come back later? It's one of the few things my little device can't help me with." She flashed her RoboHealth app and Lissa tried to conceal her instinctual eye roll.

"I tried to remove mine," Lissa said.

"Really?" The woman queried, wide-eyed, "I can't imagine how many times I would've died without it. It reminds me to take my pills, and it told me when I had a Vitamin D and calcium deficiency. This thing might've kept me from developing osteoarthritis."

"But it couldn't help you with the reason why you're here," Lissa reminded her.

"Yes. So. I think I'm dealing with some attachment issues."

"What's going on more specifically? I sense a young man around you."

The woman stared at Lissa a long time before speaking. "My teenage son. I loved him dearly, but he was a mess. Still is. And crazy as this sounds ..." She turned off her device and her phone. "I don't want it flagging me and trying to send some antipsychotic." She looked around nervously, as if someone were listening to their conversation.

"Um, well my son—he haunts me, and I want him gone."

Lissa glanced back toward the woods, where the spirit was standing, looking annoyed. She placed her hand on the woman's forearm. "I understand. Sometimes the kids hang on." The customer's eyes widened a moment, and she smiled, revealing gold caps in the back of her mouth, but the smile quickly faded. Lissa asked the woman to go on.

"He's always here with me, but it's not in a good way. I don't know why he's angry with me. Do you have any services for something like that? Like a medium? I have a few questions I'd like to ask him," she said.

"It doesn't quite work that way here, but I can walk you through the process. I can definitely tap into his energy and see what he has to say to you. You might be the one answering questions, but I have to warn you that speaking to him will only be possible if he wants to listen. They don't always want to listen."

There was a loud banging noise, and both women looked up to see nothing but trees swaying outside. One of the larger branches had just hit the window.

"Shit. Is that him?" The woman asked nervously.

"Oh, that's just our oak." Lissa waved her hand in dismissal. "I hope it never takes out our window," Lissa said.

"You sure?" the woman asked, clearly skeptical of the explanation. Lissa took a moment to smile at the woman as a sort of invitation to continue. The woman sighed, "So, tell me about how this works. Maybe you can help me at least to understand why this is happening."

Lissa smiled, feeling the left side of her mouth lift higher. "I can tap into his energy, but I need someone to watch the front of the store. Can you come back later this week? We can set an appointment for when my partner arrives," she offered.

"Sign me up. Tammy. Can I pay upfront?" The woman adjusted her hand to show purple nail polish chipping at the corners and a slim, gold pen that doubled as a light. She tapped her credit card and waited for the amount.

"It'll be $227 total." It was the largest purchase anyone had made in a week. Maybe things were picking back up.

Temperatures were over a hundred degrees with record-high humidity that evening. When Lissa felt her phone buzz, her breath caught and time stilled as she saw the Victims' Rights Notification arrive. Her phone buzzed again, and she got a similar email. Trent. She felt all the strength she'd built up buckle beneath the fear. He was being assessed and would be up for bail sooner than expected. His family could afford bail, which meant it was only a matter of time.

When her phone buzzed again, this time it was her Robo-Health app, telling her that her pulse rate was up and she should try some deep breathing. She tried, but each deep inhale seemed to get stuck. She forwarded the message to her mother and Annika.

The hazy, thick air made Lissa feel like she was walking inside an armpit. As she moved, hustling to open the shop the next day, she felt everything she'd built up in her life since leaving TLC begin to atrophy. Everything. She felt the way she had in the hospital bed.

It was as though a dark cloud descended over the shop and her life in general, just as it had when she lost her father, just as it had twenty years later—when she met Trent, and shortly thereafter her entire world was upended. This time, she had to do something.

"You'll be fine," Annika wrote.

"Do you need anything?" Pauline asked.

Lissa wrote them both. "I'm fine. I'm walking it off. I think I'm fine."

But she wasn't. She felt helpless. Should she get a restraining order? Could she? Was there a spell? And here, Lissa stopped, remembering Annika mentioning Inga a few times over the years, when they were still trying to figure out how to open the shop. Back then, before business really picked up, they'd take long walks together or huddle in cafés, where they'd sketch out plans for what they'd build and sometimes reminisce. Once, when they were in Annika's apartment, poring over small business how-to articles online, Lissa asked how magic might help their business. They'd just filed officially, and the adrenaline was palpable in the room. Annika pulled out a bottle of mead and began to shake her head. "We have to be careful with that. There's a line, and I feel like I'm still figuring it out. Caution is always best."

"Caution because you've made mistakes before?"

"Small ones, but I've been cautious because I've seen the damage a powerful witch can do. My mentor, for instance. I am trying to be that for you, and I want to do it right."

Annika said Inga, the founding member of her previous coven, had been a good friend at first. After a run of disappointments in Inga's life, including the sudden death of her only child, Inga began to practice blood magic, such as manipulation and revenge spells—starting with the drunk driver who'd killed her daughter. After one such spell, this kind of magic became addictive, according to Annika. She explained that this kind of magic gave a person too much power. The magic of manipulation is easier and faster, Annika said. It gives the illusion of control.

"Sounds like anything. The more power, the more there is at risk."

"Inga was the most powerful witch I've met," Annika said, nodding.

It was this line about power, not caution or the entire premise of that conversation that stuck with Lissa. Only the promise of magic strong enough to combat her fear. Knowing Annika would forbid her from reaching out, Lissa scoured the internet for Inga, just to get a sense for herself. Apparently, a pagan blogger named Inga lived in the area and did private consults. The only way to get in touch was to book an appointment, so after putting a $200 consultation fee on credit, Lissa had a video meeting scheduled for that evening with a jovial looking elderly woman who, according to her website photo, might as well have been Mrs. Claus.

Just before sundown, Lissa tried to ignore the whirling in her stomach as she perched on her office chair and set up her camera. She was in the Zoom waiting room for a few minutes, and when the screen finally changed, revealing Inga's face, she could immediately sense her presence. Inga stared at Lissa a long time before she nodded.

"Tell me about yourself," she said in a measured voice. As Lissa began to introduce herself, avoiding mention of Annika, Inga's look portrayed something that wasn't quite compassion. More like determination. Like she'd heard this story too many times before and was ready to dive in and help. When Lissa heard a familiar dinging sound, she was surprised to see Inga checking her RoboHealth app, the deluxe version.

"I'm surprised you use that as a witch," Lissa said.

"This thing is brilliant. I'm diabetic," Inga said.

"But aren't you worried they're used for tracking your—?"

"What isn't? Let them track me down and burn me at the stake. Let them try." She seemed to delight in her own fantasy of this. Her laugh was guttural. After a long moment, she looked directly at the screen and lowered her voice. "Talk, Lissa. You've been rambling. Tell me what you need. Say it clearly and in as few words as possible. I'm a busy person."

"I reached out because I heard of you. I practice the craft, but I'm still kind of new to everything. Only a few years in. I was beginning to feel my power, to trust myself. I feel like I'm still learning, and I have had these panic attacks lately. Nothing helps. My ex is getting out of prison. Or already out."

"Sounds like you know how to pick 'em. Then again, there are a lot of fuckwads in this world, so your odds were good."

Lissa paused before continuing. "I didn't find magic until I hit rock bottom a few years ago, after the relationship got dangerous. He's in prison because of me. He tried to kill me. Twice, really. And I was terrified of everything. This practice healed me, then it built me up, but now I feel like it—and everything I love—is in jeopardy. I feel like I'm losing myself again, just knowing he's out there."

"He's out there indeed. Go on."

"Everything was going well till I got word about him. Everything. I just need to stop worrying so much."

"Your fear is warranted, girl. It's a tale that women have known for thousands of years. Once you've met your monster, the monster keeps coming," Inga said without a smile. She powered down her phone. "What's your gift?"

"I can connect with, um, spirits. I hear them from time to time, and while I can't hear thoughts, I am very intuitive. The spirits and the messages that surround people are my way of helping people—to connect with the dead is something I'm good at, but I'm still working at fully understanding that realm. Sometimes I can share messages or just sense the messages, but that's it. I wouldn't have chosen to be a medium. I'd rather work with the upper realms, or even figure out how to work with this one, but I'm embracing my path, and I'm still learning."

"You've always been able to cross the realms?"

"What do you mean?"

"Childhood. Think, girl. Did you see things then? Hear them? Did you ever travel down there in a dream?" She pointed down for emphasis.

Lissa hadn't really thought about the voices as a gift then. More like fantasy. "I remember hearing my father after he died, and my great-grandmother who he often spoke about. She'd tell stories and sing. And this young girl who would follow my neighbor around, like a daughter. She was the first spirit I not only heard but could see, but it started to bother me after a while, and I was able to tune her out."

"Hm." She angled her body, as though looking for someone behind Lissa, which caused Lissa to turn around. "Tell me about the young girl."

"She wore a nightgown. She would hold on to the neighbor's leg, like she was trying to hold her back from something or hide. Every now and then, she'd smile, but it was always sort of reserved. I didn't know how to talk to her then."

"Your neighbor lost a child."

Lissa tried to remember her neighbor. Mrs. Marla had never divulged much about her past, and how would a thing like that come up anyway? She was a quiet, kind woman with short hair and big earrings, and she walked her two dogs three times a day, always waving to Lissa on her way home from school.

Inga cleared her throat. "Come back to me, girl. So. I've been practicing magic since you were a child seeing ghosts. I've seen enough to know that the monster you fear will keep coming for you, relentlessly. You have more power than you know, and they're attracted to that. They always keep coming. Just watch the news if you don't believe me. There are evil forces at work on this planet."

"What if I'm not powerful enough to keep him away? Or what if my power brings him to me? Like my fear is powerful too?"

Inga chuckled knowingly. "You are afraid of everything. Yourself, your ex. But you say that you know the craft. If you were a hack, you wouldn't have these childhood experiences, so, study schmudy. You're either a witch or you're not. You don't get to choose it. Now, you said you've been dedicated for a few years now. Tell me about your current practice."

"I have a mentor. Mentors, really. We practice on the moon cycles and Wheel of the Year celebrations. I've read the books—all the classics, I guess you'd say. I practice candle magic at home. Water magic at times. I'm learning about plants. At work, I help people to speak to the spirits who are hanging around. I've been able to find my deepest magic when serving my clients. I think it's because they don't know what to say, or how to say what they want to say, and I'm able to translate pretty well. Just a vision or assurance can truly change a person's life. I've seen that in them. And I cast protection spells that work. Even abundance—well, those used to work. I'm not sure now."

"Well then. Good. It seems like you have more gifts than you admit to yourself, but I want you to know that humility is overrated, and it grates on my teeth." Inga sighed loudly into her microphone.

She had on an old-school headset that amplified her voice with an echo. "Especially in women. Remember that."

"I'm just telling you how I feel. I want to feel differently," Lissa said. She searched for spirits that might be hanging on to the woman, but there was nothing. In fact, Inga had an etheric, spirit-like quality herself. She didn't seem fully in this world or of this world.

"I'm old, darling. I don't have all the time you do on this shithole planet, so let's get to it. The spell is simple if we want to eliminate him, and my assessment is that you'll do fine with the magic, but we have a little hurdle to overcome first."

"What?" Lissa noticed the owl perched on the mantel behind Inga appeared real, taxidermy maybe. She wondered if Inga had done it herself and, if so, what she'd done with the bones.

"You have the chops, and it is as easy as buttering bread, this spell. My concern is …" Lissa wondered if her pause was earnest or for dramatic effect.

"Yes?" Lissa repositioned, and as she stood, angling her computer screen up, she noticed a tiny red flicker in Inga's eye. Maybe a reflection from the camera.

"You have all this anxiety blocking your magic, all this pesky self-doubt. It's a dark red color, like clotted blood. I don't think you can snap your fingers and get rid of that, and the spells for such things take time."

"So I can't do anything?"

"You can. But it's harder. You need to either build a bridge and get over yourself, or, more likely, you'll need to pull out a little strategy. So here's the strategy. Are you ready and listening? Because I don't repeat myself."

"Yes!"

"Anxiety is a magic killer. You must distract your conscious mind. Do something to stop the anxiety temporarily, or this kind of spell will never work."

"But that's why I'm here. I don't know how to stop the anxiety."

"Same with most magic you are trying to master at home. All in vain if you don't calm down. Your mind chatter gets in the way," she said, as she made a mouth out of her fingers and opened and closed it in front of her forehead.

It seemed Inga was purposely trying to agitate Lissa. She asked again, slowly, with intention. "How do I do that?"

Inga seemed pleased. "NDE."

"NDE?"

The owl was staring at Lissa, and the way Inga was positioned now, it appeared to be sitting on her shoulder.

"Near-death experience. It's the best option for neurotic witches like yourself."

"Okaaay," Lissa said skeptically, looking at her own image in Zoom, rather than Inga's.

The older woman snapped her fingers. "Some people can make a thing like sky diving work, but I don't know if that's you. You sky dive?" Lissa shook her head. "Didn't think so. Others prefer to use drugs to mimic the effect. Mushrooms. Hallucinogens. But you never know what you're getting, even from the government."

"Especially from the government," Lissa agreed.

Inga continued. "Orgasm can work sometimes, too, but it must be a big one." She extended her hands as though holding a large ball.

"What does that even mean?" Lissa said, softening a little, amused at the thought of a measurable orgasm. She wondered if the health apps could do that.

"Experiment, girl."

"What about meditations? I read …"

"Meditation works if you have a few years to spare, but magic will work as fast as that. You took years to let all that juicy anxiety build in your system, so a temporary fix and slow. I guess if you have time to spare. So. Take your pick, then the magic will work like it's supposed to."

"Um—what if I can't distract my conscious mind? And what kind of spell is this? Also, what do you mean by get rid of him? I don't want to kill him or anything. I just want him to stay away from me."

"We can't concern ourselves with definitions, and you don't get to choose. The natural law will determine all of that, and it is curious to see if you'll follow through. What I can guarantee is that if you can follow my instructions, you will get what you need out of this spell. Whatever that means is none of your business. Once you cast, it's out of your control."

"Is there a spell to make him get arrested again?"

"Are you listening? Magic operates under natural law. The legal system does not. The two will never work well together." Inga was getting bored with this conversation, reading her app notifications. "Also, it's kinda mean to lock a human up in a cage, don't ya think?" Inga added, looking up with a defiant smile, as though entertaining herself. She wore a light pink blouse with a frilled collar, and Lissa wondered about her day-to-day life. She imagined Inga bringing blueberry muffins out to her mailperson and giving a card to the woman who worked at the grocery. She might be the neighborhood gossip, or the power-walking elderly lady of her block.

"I guess I'm not worried about being mean," Lissa said at last.

"Right! This is self-defense," Inga said. "It's for the greater good."

Lissa tried to tune into Inga's surroundings and could only imagine her in either a mansion on the north side of town or a trailer on the south side—nothing in the middle. According to Annika, she had been busy rebuilding her coven with younger witches after destroying the sanctity of the last one. Lissa couldn't help but wonder if she'd been reading her mind. If she'd cursed Annika with such an ability, there was likelihood that she herself could tap into others' thoughts, too.

"Want it or not?"

"Yes." Having paid the $200 consultation fee, Lissa figured she might as well take the offered spell.

"Excellent," Inga said. "I'll send it in an encrypted file now."

When Lissa saw the .docx arrive in the chat section of Zoom, hardly an encrypted file, she felt her skepticism showing and tried to relax her eyebrows. Sure she'd been scammed, she wrote down the simple chant Inga gave her, along with the instructions that she was to recite it three times, with a visualization that must be done either when in deep meditation or with a distracted conscious mind. How could that possibly work? It was too simplistic and seemed utterly ridiculous. No candles, no complex rituals or waiting on the moon to wane. Just a few words in the middle of a heightened experience.

"This is it?" she asked.

"This is it. Tell Annika I said hello," Inga said, smiling for the first time with teeth.

"How'd you—?"

"I miss that girl. Sad she got so full of herself and hived off the way she did, but I suppose it's the natural course of things. I hear she's a high priestess now. You know, her magic was nothing when she met me. I was her mentor, like she is yours. Tell her I don't blame her for leaving Kat, though. That girl spiraled, but I'm getting her back on track."

"What do—?"

Inga was not concerned with Lissa's questions anymore. She concluded the session in a firm voice, her finger pointing toward the screen and gaze fixed, with that hint of red reflecting near her pupil. "You deserve your freedom, remember that. Don't worry about what's right. This world has no true moral compass. We witches are here to fix that, and Annika is still learning this lesson. Maybe you can help her one day. Now, go demand your freedom!"

Lissa stared at the woman's honey-colored eyes and chubby cheeks, noticing the way they softened and settled into something more grandmother-like again. "Thank you," she started to say, but the screen went black.

Annika

Annika had a dream that Trent would be released before Lissa got word of it. After losing landscaping clients and finding his business near ruin, he'd start drinking more often, just like his father had. She saw him deciding it was all Lissa's fault after all. His dreams would collect dust in his mother's garage, and he'd come barreling down I-71 with no other intention than to get his revenge.

When she woke, she realized her friend's safety, maybe even her life, might be in jeopardy again. Lissa, too, had claimed to have nightmares from time to time, and her magic was getting stronger, which coincided with her intuition. Trent would be up for bail soon, and Annika knew she'd have to intervene.

Sitting straight up in bed, she glanced over at the mirror. Her hair was already getting a few gray strands, the result of hearing too many thoughts over the years, and she wondered if she could get away with never leaving home again. She wondered about this daily. The quietude of her own space was the most peace she ever got.

Walking barefoot toward the kitchen, causing creaks in the wooden floorboards, she paused at her oven and placed a pot of water on the range, turning the flame all the way up and grabbing a strainer and two large bags of loose-leaf tea—lavender and rosemary—to prep her mug.

Her back window faced a small field near the train tracks, and some mornings she'd delight in the chugging sound of the freight making its way west. Now, it was not yet 5 a.m. The darkness suited her, and after allowing her tea to steep, she placed the strainer in the pot, which was still full of hot water, and she started a ritual bath. Her fridge, which was full of goat's milk for handmade soap, contained little food, so she toasted some bread and smothered it with homemade rose jelly as she watched a series of swallows glide by the window and asked them what to do. When she didn't get an answer, she dumped the pot of water in her bath, allowing the lavender to heighten her senses and the rosemary to offer clarity as she remained open to answers.

True magic works on its own timeline, so as Annika's skin began to wrinkle and the water cooled, she began moving with a bit more expediency. She adorned her eyes with jet black liner before setting up her space. As she thumbed through her closet of black, gray and purple clothes—a bit cliché, she admitted—she envisioned a thick pink ring of light around her, a protective energy field, then threw on a tight pair of black leggings and a tank top beneath the shimmery, see-through sweater Lissa had given her for her birthday last year.

Lighting a candle to Morrigan, the goddess who most spoke to her when she was alone, Annika said a prayer asking for clarity and stood to watch the flame as she drank her last sip of tea. Still nothing. Perhaps the dream was only that. Paranoia because she loved her friend. But even the thought of this seemed off. The timelines felt off, everything just a little too slow, and she double checked to make sure there was no daylight savings change she'd forgotten about.

Like clockwork, the answer arrived just as she forgot to wait for it—while cutting someone off as she quickly merged into rush hour traffic. By the time she arrived at the shop, the entire plan was mapped out in her mind.

"Seems slow," she said, giving Lissa a one-armed hug.

"Yep. Again."

Annika noticed that Lissa was scrambling to close her phone. She'd been checking Trent's social media again, which was being run by his mother while he was inside, and she tried to hide it, despite knowing well enough that Annika could hear her thoughts. Lissa had adopted the habit of thinking quickly about ice cream when she remembered Annika could hear her. It was rather funny at first but was getting old.

"How about we switch it up, Lissa? Puppies or something?"

Lissa's face fell as she tried her best to look annoyed. "Fine, I'll think of puppies when you're invading my head space."

To ensure her friend was safe, Annika had decided that Trent needed to realize for himself that he was the one in control of his actions. There was no one to blame. She'd have to give him hope. She could write him—maybe she'd say she was a guy who'd been where he was, lost it all and still succeeded. Or a cute college student who was empathetic with his plight. After all, what else would Trent have to do in prison but read letters and imagine some pretty sorority sister on the other side?

"Since we're slow, can you watch the shop a little longer?" she asked Lissa.

"No problem. Can you pick me up lunch?" Lissa asked. "Glad you're finally wearing that," she added, nodding to the sweater.

"It's shiny," Annika said in mock disgust, then rushed off. Lissa always wanted the same things: a salmon salad or a tuna salad sandwich, and Annika used to joke that she harnessed the power of mercurial energy. After walking a few blocks to the post office and standing in line an hour, Annika tried the tiny key to her new PO Box. While she was waiting for Lissa's lunch, she wrote the first letter.

Dear Trent,

I'm working on my master's degree in English, and one of my assignments this semester is to return to the epistolary form, the art of letters if you will. I know that I don't know you, but I saw your case in the paper. I'm from Indiana. I might be able to offer you some company. Maybe a little perspective.

I was a double major in undergrad—sociology and writing, and I learned a lot in my sociology classes about prison dynamics. It makes me wonder a lot about you. What was your home life like? How has prison changed you? Has it?

This is too many questions. Let me tell you a little about me. Believe it or not, my parents were perfect. Who can say that, right? Neither of them beat me or anything. We had food and got to go camping. I was in band and Spanish club. I even went to Spain my senior year of high school. Yes, it was a private school. You probably know the one.

I'm writing you for this assignment, but I'm also writing because I think I understand you more than you can imagine. Despite everything in my life going well, I started to get this rage during the Covid-19 pandemic. It was wild. I felt like the whole world was closing in, and for me being a college student, about to graduate with my undergraduate degree, I missed out on all the things a senior is supposed to do. It didn't feel fair, and it didn't feel like the world supported me, and I wanted people to listen. Do you know what? Those closest to me didn't hear me at all. They didn't care about my pain. I worked so incredibly hard, and they didn't care.

I feel like you work hard too. The local paper said you built up your family's land-scaping company to what it was pretty much single handedly. You're like a celebrity all throughout Indiana and even into Ohio. That shows a crazy work ethic.

I want to write books, a little different, but trust me when I say it's harder work than you think. Anyway, I just wanted to introduce myself and let you know you're not alone. I have holes in my walls to prove that I can relate to losing my temper from time to time. But women are lucky. We're not strong enough to do any real damage, so we never get into too much trouble.

What women are good at though—we're good at seeing things as they are, and I can tell you that when you get out, things will be better out here. I have hope. This pandemic is clearing up, and I've been reading a lot of essays about the stoics and how to move forward and create your own version of reality. I'm including one of the essays I read recently in this letter. I think you might find it interesting. It's on Aristotle's Golden Mean theory. Sending you well wishes in there. I'll make the next letter a little more interesting. Tell you a little more about me, but I want to make sure you're going to write back first. Please write back. I could use a pen pal.

Hayley

She reread her work. "Who would believe they'd get a fan letter in prison from a girl dropping vague details in an adoring tone after you beat the shit out of your wife?" Annika asked aloud as she added the signature at the deli table. The man behind the counter made a confused sound. "A man who thinks the world revolves around him, that's who." The worker placed the white carryout bag in front of her and backed away.

A week later, Annika began checking the PO Box, and though it took longer than expected, eventually a letter came. Reading it, she could tell he'd restarted it a few times. The spelling was impeccable, and he'd thrown in a few academic words that were totally unnecessary. Annika had never met Trent outside of the time she'd had to fight him off her friend, but she knew his type. And she played to every dream he had, reading deeper into each letter, and disliking him more with each word.

She wrote weekly those last months, never telling Lissa, and when he started to say that he was going to be up for bail soon, she played up how unique an opportunity this was to start over and really build his business. The vision she'd had of him coming after Lissa had been steadily fading, and she was confident that she'd done her work. Trent was going to be taken care of. He would have new goals now, new ambitions—new delusions, sure, but they'd be distracting enough.

Toward the end of the year, when Lissa called her, panicked, she tried to talk sense into her. "I promise he's not going to bother you if he gets out," she said, and when Lissa didn't listen, Annika worried that all her work had been in vain. This hadn't been magic, it'd been a chess move, and now she had to convince her friend not to use magic against him. That kind of magic ruined lives in ways anxiety couldn't touch.

When Lissa arrived at the shop some weeks later, just before Tren was about to be released, Annika was holding a piece of quartz, and she watched her friend intently, with a knowing smile, finally ready to share the news that she was sure Trent would leave her be. She heard her friend's thoughts loud and clear. Inga.

After all Annika had done for Lissa, she couldn't listen to one simple instruction, and Annika wasn't sure she could forgive. The hurt that came with trust, with love, had arrived. This wasn't how it was supposed to go, but it was how it went.

Lissa tried to rationalize, but Annika put her foot down. "No. You know I don't condone that kind of magic. It always comes back, and it comes back in every way. That one visit to Inga is probably why business is down. It's the downfall of more than you can imagine."

"That sounds a little dramatic," Lissa said.

"Dramatic?"

"I mean, she didn't even seem legit. And it doesn't make sense, Annika," Lissa said, but Annika fumed. She thought about all they had been through to rehabilitate and how much her friend had thrown away with one stupid decision. The countless nights she'd stayed up late with Lissa, sharing her Book of Shadows, her secrets, teaching her about plants and herbs. Writing her asshole ex-husband for all these months to ensure he wouldn't mess with her.

"You should've come to me. You didn't. You made your choice, and honestly, I don't know if I can be your friend anymore."

"You don't mean that," Lissa said. "I was scared, but I haven't used the spell. It'll be fine."

"You have no idea. It's never fine with Inga. And I was already … never mind. Just give me some space."

Annika needed more than space from Lissa. She cast a spell that invited in a spirit of protection. Someone or something that would take earthly form and watch over her friend, because she'd be damned if she was going to keep doing it. Lissa didn't deserve to practice magic with their coven anymore. She'd crossed over, and though love was love, Annika would not stay in a destructive relationship.

"Goddess, I call upon thee. Bless Lissa with a familiar to watch over her during this time of weakness." A soft brushing sound arrived at the door, and Annika went toward it. "Funny, universe. Guess I'm turning in early today."

She let the cat in and closed the shop to buy a litter box and food. Lissa was scheduled to open the next day, and the charts showed business was destined to be light for the next month. The cat mewed, and Annika bent down over it. "You're going to try to kill me, aren't you?" It batted at her cheek, and she was surprised not to be sneezing. That would probably come later. "I'm allergic to you, you know. But I thank you for coming. You've got a big job ahead."

The cat was a dark gray and rather young, probably only a few months old. It rushed to the counter and hopped up on the glass, leaving wet paw prints all over, its tail moving like a snake. Annika smiled. They were about to go on a journey. She knew that it'd be tough. Everything would have to burn for her friend to rebuild, so she called the cat Ash.

NDE
Monday, October 25

"You have to stop ignoring me, Annika.** I haven't done anything. I just had a simple conversation. To be honest, I think she swindled me," Lissa said, worried Annika would never speak to her again after a twenty-minute Zoom call.

"You did something. Just by reaching out to her, you fucking did something!" she yelled.

Annika had banned Lissa from the group magic they'd been planning to practice at Samhain, Lissa's favorite holiday celebration, during which they honored the ancestors. It was her yearly opportunity to reconnect with her father, even if only in her mind. Most Samhain rituals included a dinner and honoring of the dead; it was a reverent time, and an opportunity to receive messages from the other side. This year, Lissa had been hoping she might be chosen to lead the ceremony. Now that was stripped from her, just when she needed the connection most. She'd be relegated to practicing by herself or searching online for a witchy meet-up event.

She thought about calling Doreen and Glenda, asking them to fight for her, but thought better of it. Annika would calm down in time. But Lissa feared the few skills she'd built up casting spells and reconnecting to what was previously dormant inside her would fade away for good if she didn't have support. As would the shattered parts of her confidence that remained, and her one true friendship.

After a few days passed, things got worse. Annika refused to speak to Lissa, explaining she needed to "process," and the few words she did speak amounted to whatever was necessary to keep the business running.

But you know how dangerous Trent is. You know how desperate I am not to lose what we've built. She would plead in her mind with Annika, but her friend seemed to ignore her thoughts.

It was the day of Trent's release, and a strong autumn wind

almost claimed Lissa's keycard as she scanned the empty parking lot before unlocking the front door of the office building. She secured her pepper spray, stopping at a purple door bearing a small plaque with TSH inscribed in gold letters. The back lights had been left on in the suite, and the familiar smell of cardamom-vanilla incense lingered in the room as the security warning hummed.

After she typed in the security code, the hum turned into a beep, then went silent. When she flipped the audio, soft guitar music began, then display lights illuminated the crystals near the side window. She noticed a subtle sweeping sound coming from the back and took cautious steps toward the back room. Something brushed her ankle. As she jumped back, a small gray cat pranced around her feet, batting a paw at a neatly folded piece of paper.

"Who are you?" she asked the cat, and it dashed toward the back room again. Lissa paused by the display cases filled with handmade jewelry, athames, spell kits, and a variety of collectible esoteric books, noticing that the trash cans hadn't been emptied, and a kombucha bottle had been left near the register. Because unexpected visitors were nothing new to The Spirit House, she took her time digesting the fact that there was a furry new arrival, perhaps a spirit himself, and she made a kissing sound to coax him out. The cat's head peeked around the corner, then retreated.

"Come on, buddy," Lissa said, noticing the slight tugging sensation in her jaw as she smiled. The cat darted its head out again, then took a few slow steps toward her. It was no apparition or visitor from the spirit realm. This cat was 3D, as was the letter it had been playing with on the floor. After extending her hand for a few curious sniffs, Lissa and the cat each decided the other was trustworthy enough. She reached for the paper.

It read 14 Days. The exact number of days she and Annika were late on rent. A week ago, when the landlord called, Lissa had been sure she'd have the funds within a day, and so her lie hadn't been intentional. According to that month's astrological chart, business was supposed to pick up. Abundance was flowing her way. Mercury was in opposition to Saturn, and the years-long recession after the pandemic was finally lifting. On top of all that, a new customer was supposed to buy the foot-tall lingam stone that sat in the display near the front. All signs pointed toward a deluge, but no one came, and the high-dollar customer said she'd come back next week.

Then, like a wave, there'd been a record number of cancellations and false promises, and those who happened to walk in the store were the less desirable customers—those who were waiting to see the cosmetic dentist or, worse, the lawyer in an adjacent and identical building. Such people wandered around aimlessly, picking things up and putting them down, or asking about the shop's services with mild disinterest, only to say they'd be back later.

Lissa wondered if Annika had been right and Inga had somehow cursed them, but this seemed too illogical. Even magic had its limits, she thought. And besides, her intentions had been to simply stay safe, not to hurt anyone. She hadn't used the spell.

14 Days. She turned the note over, wondering if things could truly get worse. Her landlord, Julianne O'Malley, was a widow and a mother of four who owned most of the commercial property in the arts district. A driven businessperson with conservative beliefs, Lissa remembered her reluctancy to allow a metaphysical store in this suite anyway, a reluctance that was overridden by Annika's ability to produce two months' rent in advance. O'Malley probably had one of her children write a creepy note on the way to daycare to save time.

Lissa modified the note by folding it in half and adding Sale: above 14 Days, then placed the thick paper in the front of the crystal display that faced the front door as she recalled the excitement of opening this business with Annika four years ago, when it seemed they couldn't fail.

But the novelty of TSH for this small-town Ohio neighborhood wore off, and now, after a year of barely making rent, Lissa knew that the first warning was also the last. More than a few startups were waiting for this space, including a Botox clinic that would surely never be late on rent.

To make matters worse, most businesses in the building were thriving, but as an economist on NPR had recently said, the wellness bubble was now a bust. Robots and health apps offered the logical solutions most consumers preferred. Plant-based medications tweaked in a lab were more precise and convenient than the messages from ancestors to go on pilgrimages or the subtle but more responsible magic TSH could offer. Lissa had been doing endless recitations of her prosperity mantra, lighting carved candles and inviting in the support of her guides, but she was still waiting on the results. No sugar bowl magic or spell seemed to work anymore. And while Annika was powerful as ever, Lissa's partner refused to use magic for some strange reason.

"I don't understand your mom," Lissa called in response to

the faint mewing from the back room. She found her place behind the counter and stared outside, watching the trees sway. She started to dial Annika's number to inquire about the cat, but the phone slipped out of her hand and onto the glass case. The contents of her purse were coated in travel lotion from a flattened bottle. She remembered sitting down hard on her purse during her graceless entry into the Uber that morning. She swabbed the lotion off and stared at her reflection in the greasy screen, attempting a smile and revealing the slight dimples her mother gave her, but her eyes were tired. "You are part of Divine Source," she reminded herself before wiping down the contents of her purse: a wallet, two cans of pepper spray, a taser, and a half-eaten protein bar that was a week old but looked salvageable. There was no hair tie.

She was about to dial again when the cat raced toward her, then stopped short and waited. Lissa wondered if she should open the hall door and let him run out. There were plenty of strays in the neighborhood, so it wasn't too surprising that one had made his way in the building. Annika must've seen him nosing around the hall and decided to let him into the store.

"I guess I don't blame her. You're a cutie—but why did she leave you here?" she asked the cat, moving her thick dark hair to one side as she retrieved a sample bottle of lavender oil and added six drops to the diffuser. The cat purred and jumped up on the counter next to her, mewing and strutting as though trying to get her attention. It hit her hair, then side-eyed the questionable contents of her purse, which made Lissa shrug. "Can't be too safe, buddy. I have enemies. Maybe it is overkill." Her fingers traced his collar to find a small tag that read, "Ash."

"You have a home?" she asked the cat, who gave her a steadfast gaze, then tilted his head as though to say This is my home, silly.

Lissa stared back at the hazel eyes and wondered if this cat's presence meant she was violating code. Another reason for O'Malley to kick them out. Riverpark, once a wasteland near Akron, Ohio, was being renovated at hyper-speeds, and this meant there'd also likely be increases and tighter regulations every year. Lissa lit a money-drawing candle and one that offered a fiery wall of protection.

Ash headbutted her bag, almost knocking it into the candles. "Be careful! Geesh. If you're squatting here, do you have a litter box at least?"

The cat looked around, then followed Lissa around as though

he, too, would like to know. A small bowl of water and a paper plate with crusted-over wet food sat near the storage closet, in the perfect place for Lissa to knock it over. It wasn't until she arrived at the back room, amongst the backstock of crystals and oils they'd ordered when the shop had been thriving, that she found the cat box hidden behind the door. Ash mewed and stared up at Lissa, as though politely excusing her, and Lissa acquiesced, keeping the door cracked so that the kitty could get back to his food. She sent Annika a simple text. "Can you tell me about your cat?"

By lunchtime, no one had stopped in, so Lissa reread a book on aromatherapy and tried to distract herself from the wave of unease that used to arrive at 1 p.m. every day and now marked Trent's release. The darkness was strongest during the quiet times, the calm days. Before she'd owned the shop or had any gainful work of her own during the pandemic, 1 p.m. was the time when her ex-husband would arrive home from work. She never knew which version of Trent would walk through the door—exhausted or enraged. Either way, he'd turn off all the lights, close the blackout curtains to alleviate his perpetual headache, then plop down on the couch with his balding head resting in his hands, or he would interrogate her about her day and grumble about business.

Lissa eyed the door of the shop, imagining the heavy footfall she used to hear. The sound of his keys dropping on the glass table. Instinctually, she reached for the place near her ear where her scar began and traced it down to her collar bone and felt herself there again. She knew when she felt panic like this, she was supposed to visualize her safe place or recite a song of safety, but instead, she stood alert, as though preparing for battle. She tried to count down from ten and breathe through the fear. But it wasn't that easy. He might already be free, ready to enact his retaliation for imprisonment.

She reached for her purse as she waited for the panic to subside, trying to focus on the music, a light drumming now accompanying the soft guitar when she heard the buzz of her phone. Expecting to see a response from Annika, instead she saw a series of new messages from her mother, Pauline.

Message 1: "How are you doing?"
Message 2: "I'm getting you something."
Message 3: "You might not like it."
Message 4: "I hope you're doing okay. I know we're having dinner together soon, but I haven't seen you since the news about—"

Message 5: "I want you to know I'm here."

Lissa didn't answer. Instead, she focused on relaxing, calling in her guides. She glanced out the side window to catch a glimpse of someone walking toward her, in the direction of the building's back door. Hoping it was Annika, terrified it was Trent, she stepped forward and saw, instead, a tall redhead who worked across the street at a law firm. Lissa couldn't help but think that a woman like this would never have to endure the trauma and shame Lissa lived with every day, the trauma that had been amplified since Trent's impending release.

As though hearing her, the redhead paused to look toward the tiny window. Her waxy lips lifted at one corner as she caught Lissa's deer-like stare. The woman briefly examined the small display of crystals and oracle cards visible from the window, but just as Lissa lifted her hand to wave her in, the woman quickly turned to catch stride with a brunette waiting ahead.

"I'm OK, I'm OK," she said, watching the confident stride of the two women. She turned back to the cat. "That's the kind of customer we need to manifest, Ash. Those ladies could buy the lingam stone and not think twice." The cat meowed, as if in reply.

Lissa hadn't focused her studies of magic, but she soon would. For her, the last years had been like a foundational education and the various rituals gave her structure and grounding. But nothing in this moment worked the same as it used to. She tried to muster the feeling she'd had when it was new, when she first met Annika and it seemed everything was aligning. But no magic seemed accessible in the same way. Lissa's nana, her father, and other spirit guides weren't audible to her beneath the constant screech of anxiety that took up residence in her head now.

She knew Trent's freedom was the reason everything in her life had been falling apart—relationships, business, and equilibrium. It couldn't be Inga. Inga had told her what seemed true. Her fear was sapping her magic, her autonomy. And now she was even losing the magic that had saved her. She began to count again but was interrupted by a loud crashing sound.

Pauline

Blue's Pawn Shop smelled vaguely of cigar smoke and musky cologne. Pauline leaned over the menacing-looking handgun laying atop the glass cabinet.

"9 mm Glock. Any more questions, I'll try my best to answer," the man behind the counter said. He kept looking down at his phone each time Pauline asked something, and she was pretty sure he'd been Googling the answers he'd given so far. Either way, he was kind and thorough enough, so she didn't mind. She didn't have any questions left, not logical ones, but she asked nonetheless: "Is it safe?"

He stared at her for a long time. "I don't know how to answer that honestly other than to say no, but if you have any other questions …"

Pauline was curious about this answer. Wasn't he here to sell things? "No, no. You've been a doll. Thanks for showing me so many. Can you hold this one for a week? I think the size is good. I have to figure out the best way to gift it, and I just want a few days to think."

"This isn't for you, huh?"

I don't have a psychopath for an ex-husband, she thought. "No, not for me. My daughter. She needs protection. I'm not sure how to present it to her, though. Do you gift wrap?"

The man appeared as though he was trying not to smile. "No. But I hope this will bring her peace, Ma'am. Could I have your cell number?"

Pauline felt a little flutter in her chest, and she was grateful for the shift inside her. She looked beyond the sweet-faced man to the mirrored glass case behind him that held expensive jewelry and collectibles and appreciated her own reflection before smiling slowly. She hadn't been flirted with in a while, and she played along even though she felt a little too sophisticated for this guy. Today, she had to admit, she looked good. She wore all black and her sleekest pair of dark-framed glasses, which sat close enough to her face that her long lashes tickled the lenses. "Now what would you want that for—um, …?"

"Lee." He looked confused a moment, then straightened his shoulders. "Well, I could call you to, um, take you out? Somewhere nice. You like steak?"

"No."

"Whatever you want, then. A nice vegan meal. A grilled cheese. Whatever."

"It's been a hell of a few weeks. How about a martini? And a salad," she said, giving him the look she used to give Lissa when she wouldn't eat her peas. She hadn't intended to give him that look, but it was all she could think to do.

"Whatever you want." Lee was smiling now. His short-cropped beard was a silvery gray, and while he had a bit of a rough look to him, his smile was kind. "A salad and some margaritas."

Snapping to the present, Pauline straightened. "See, you lost me," she sighed, shaking her head. "You don't listen, Lee. Men never do. I'll think about it. I'll give you my number for the hold."

"Fine. Margarita for me, martini for you." Lee stood a little taller, waiting, hopeful.

"I'll think about it," Pauline repeated. She looked around the shop. Some shelves were completely bare, which made her think the place wouldn't be here for much longer. While tech businesses, medical, and other choice industries were thriving, it seemed small businesses were struggling everywhere she looked. Not that she'd ever return to the pawn shop after this purchase, Pauline thought, but it was disheartening, nonetheless. This guy probably had no job security, yet here he was, asking her out. "Thank you, Lee. Tell the owner his shop smells like smoke. Might bring more people in if you freshen it up. Get some music going." She turned on her heel.

"It's my shop for now, so I'll keep that in mind," he called after her.

"Talk soon, Lee." Pauline sauntered out, waggling her fingers behind her as she left. She was feeling a little better about the idea of giving Lissa added security. And sure, she'd turned Lee down, but the adrenaline from flirting and the whole context of the pawn shop and handgun made her feel like she was in a movie. She looked left to right as though surveying the place for bad guys. When she was younger, Pauline's favorite movie had been *Point of No Return* with Brigid Fonda, and she indulged her version of one more badass female assassin eye scan before unlocking her Subaru and driving to Lissa's apartment well below the speed limit, as usual.

The gun wasn't an ideal solution, but Lissa was in danger, and the taser Pauline had purchased for her daughter a month ago didn't feel like enough. Thirty percent of people in the country owned a gun, and though Pauline knew her daughter wouldn't like the gift, the girl might need it. Anything at all to keep her daughter safe.

Pauline took a deep breath and her mind, like a telescope, shifted to the image of the man at the pawn shop. She smiled. Life had been so quiet since Michael had died and Lissa met Trent.

As she stopped the car at her mailbox, Pauline wondered, briefly, if she should give the pawn shop owner a chance after all. Finding nothing but adverts in the box, she navigated her circular drive and headed toward the recycling bin. A pawn shop owner wasn't exactly her type, and Lee's five o'clock shadow and smoker's voice, not to mention his slightly protruding belly, weren't strong selling points.

Pauline could use some company, and Lee … well, he was rough around the edges, sure, but that could be interesting, and if the date was horrible, she'd never have to see him again. After all her years of learning to read people, she didn't get a single red flag from this guy, aside from his questionable diet and profession. Still, everyone had a narrative, and Pauline was curious about his.

"Speaking of needing company," she told herself, shaking off these ridiculous thoughts. She powered on her cellphone, which she'd had off since she left this morning, and dialed Dr. Cal Gregory's number with a surge of surety in her chest.

She hadn't been a perfect mother in the past, but Pauline was going to make up for it now that she was retired. Her daughter wasn't going to end up paranoid, or alone like her mother. And she sure as hell wasn't going to end up with some psychopath again. She was going to end up with someone who worshipped her. Someone who had empathy and a kind heart.

The young man who'd taken over Pauline's role at the Horizons Mental Health Center, Cal, had a bare left finger and a big heart. He'd been one of Michael's students when Michael used to guest lecture at Ohio State University. When they all first met at a dinner party, Cal had showered Pauline with praise over the paper she'd had published on alternate identities as a trauma response, which had truly been her life's work, having stemmed from her dissertation. She worried now sometimes that Lissa displayed aspects of creating a persona, one filled with magical thinking, as a response to abuse. But, of course, her concern wasn't something she could discuss with Cal.

The thought of introducing Cal to Lissa arrived like lightning, but the opportunity never came. Then later, when Cal said he was moving to Akron and looking for work, just around the time Pauline was entertaining the idea of retiring, she knew he was a godsend. Maybe a logical thinker could balance Lissa out, help her to reconnect.

After Pauline began training Cal, she found out he was dating an artist and model, but their relationship was strained. He confided that she'd go weeks without calling him when she was on site. It was a shame. He was brilliant and compassionate, a champion of women—everything Trent had pretended to be.

After retirement, when Pauline turned over many of her most difficult clients to Cal, she didn't get a single complaint. One particularly needy client, Ms. Jonson, who'd let out a primal scream after Pauline announced her retirement, even reached out to her old emergency line to share how much she appreciated being placed in good hands. Pauline had specialized in paranoid personality disorder and complex post-traumatic stress for over two decades, and she knew she wasn't the easiest to replace because of her specialization in this area. So when, at lunch shortly before her retirement party, Cal mentioned that the artist was moving to London, Pauline couldn't conceal her joy. That day, Pauline tried to explain away her smile over a bowl of noodles, staring at the young man's wide lapis eyes and slightly overgrown brows. "You'll find the perfect person. Only you could've done such a brilliant job with my clients. This work is not for the thin-skinned. It gets emotionally taxing, but you seem so calibrated."

"I've been studying mindfulness since undergrad," Cal said. "It's no panacea, but it helps. Dr. Mike really introduced me to it."

Pauline felt her heart swell at the mention of her husband's name. "Well I'm here for you if you ever need to talk to someone who understands," she said.

When Pauline was advancing in the field, the concept of mindfulness or meditation as a supplementary therapy was peripheral. She'd white-knuckled through for years, stomaching the perpetual anguish she saw on her patients' faces as they struggled to explain what, to Pauline, didn't need words. She'd been out of the office for over a month when they'd had that last lunch, and she still missed the work but was relieved to have a little peace between 8 a.m. and 4 p.m. weekdays and felt gratitude every day to be free of the complex emotional ties.

"It's been a while since we met up," Pauline texted Cal. She said she'd like to take him out to dinner soon as a token of appreciation for making her retirement so smooth now that he was settled in. It'd been almost two months since they had lunch at the Ramen Company.

"If you are in danger or having thoughts of self-harm, call 911 or the emergency medical number below; otherwise, I will get back to you as soon as I can," the automated response replied.

Pauline thought a moment, then sent a third message. "I'd love to introduce you to my daughter," she wrote, remembering how he'd commented on the picture of Lissa that used to sit on Pauline's desk. He'd used the word "radiant."

Less than a minute later, a response came in. "Only if it's my treat, Dr. Williams."

"Deal. Let's meet at the Grandview Inn this Thursday."

The adrenaline, coupled with anticipation of the rich food later that week, inspired Pauline to reset her health app and connect it to her new RoboHealth device—a present Lissa had given her last year that utilized some of the early ideas in her father's literature. Her blood sugar was a little low, since it had no record of her eating since this morning, but aside from that it seemed the perfect time to walk, it suggested with a thumbs-up next to the image of a walking figure alongside a few affirmations she was to repeat to herself.

Pauline quickly changed into a pink sweatsuit with a thick gray stripe up each side and began to powerwalk. But something took over today, and despite the health app's suggestion to take things easy, she began to jog, then run. By the time she reached the end of her street, she was in the closest thing to a sprint she'd been since she'd entered that one triathlon with Michael that had almost killed her. The thought of him made her run faster, and as she reached Hudson Street, she felt like nothing in the world could stop her momentum. The app paused the music to say, "Please remember to replenish your fluids in the next hour."

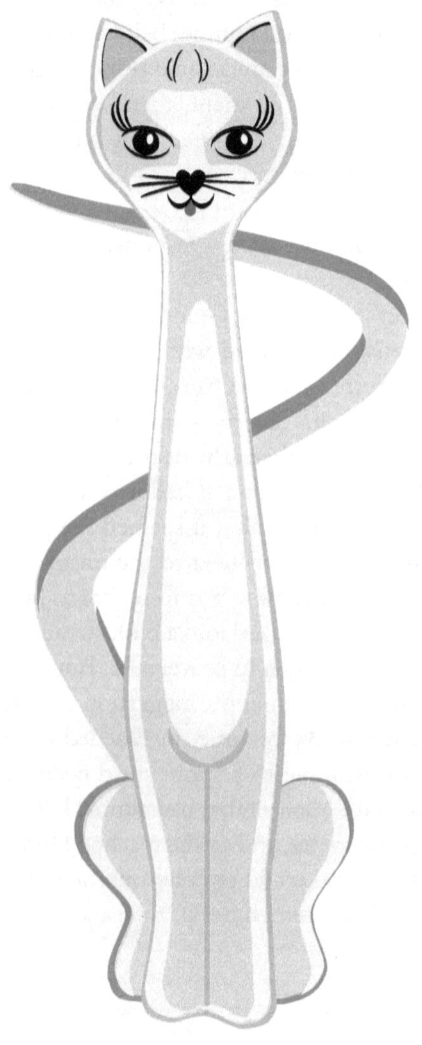

Lissa

Lissa's palms tingled. "I can't keep living like this, Ash. I can't," she said as the cat sniffed the tangy liquid and recoiled. Grabbing a natural vinegar cleanser, Lissa tried to focus on cleaning the drink that was probably a few days from becoming vinegar itself. She listened to the music, the trees, the crystals, but her mind was racing. Something inside Lissa knew that if she wanted closure from her past again, she'd have to delete it all, like a computer file. She needed stronger magic.

When she checked the appointment schedule to see Tammy's name written in her notes, she felt a bit of relief. The woman in snakeskin with her aggressive teenage ghost might be a nice distraction. Lissa settled on a stool behind the crystal display and checked her phone. There were messages from Pauline.

Message 1: "Dr. Gregory, my replacement (remember, I told you about him?), is going to come to dinner with us this Thursday, and he is extremely excited to meet you. I think you two will really hit it off. Be there at 4:45 so we can get a good seat. I want to make sure they don't try to put us next to the kitchen or under those annoying lights near the back."

Message 2: "Wear a dress. I know you don't like dresses, but they look so adorable on you, those summer dresses you have, not the muumuu. But no jeans! You always wear those same jeans. Just promise me you won't wear those jeans."

The jeans were teal blue. Lissa had gotten them in Ireland, when she'd gone on her honeymoon eight years ago, a lifetime ago, and they were one of the few articles of clothing that she'd kept from those years. Trent hadn't wanted her to buy them and admonished her every time she tried to wear them when they were together, but they were the first item she'd packed up those years ago. Skinny jeans looked good with any oversized shirt in her closet (most of the shirts in her closet were oversized), and who didn't have a favorite pair of jeans?

Response: "Mom, I will wear what I want to wear, and I can't even think about that right now. I look forward to meeting your friend (your boyfriend?)."

Message 3: A video message this time, featuring Lissa's mom with an intense expression and a colorful scarf, pulling the phone in. "Fine. Wear the jeans. No, he's too young for me." She winked. "Remember when I told you about him a long time ago? He had the artist girlfriend who didn't appreciate him. A student of your father's?" The message restarted, and Lissa watched the whole thing again, trying to remember.

When Annika came in, only about five minutes late, she didn't say hello or offer any small talk. She didn't acknowledge a text Lissa had sent her earlier asking when she'd be there. Instead, she looked at all the prosperity candles and rolled her eyes.

"We got a customer coming in," Lissa said. "Her son is haunting her."

Annika nodded.

"The info's in the books."

Still, Annika was silent. She took off her coat.

"You don't have to speak to me, but please clean your cat box," Lissa said, heading into her reading room.

Annika smiled as she whispered, "That's what she said." This broke the silence.

Lissa laughed, hoping the joke was a gesture toward forgiveness, but Annika smiled at her own joke without looking up. She was simply amusing herself. Sighing, Lissa placed the cards on the table next to a large selenite stone. She adjusted the wooden chair and turned the wooden angel, who sat in the window, to face east before checking the back for the spirit, which must've followed his mother. Lissa closed the curtains.

She hadn't done a reading in a little while, so she dusted lightly and waited, summoning the energy to be present and protected and to offer to others what she couldn't find herself. She visualized a bright pink light pulsing in the room, guarding it, and a more subtle black light around her own body for protection. When she heard Annika greet the woman pleasantly and direct her back, a slight tingle of nerves arrived, as it did with each new client.

"This room feels good," the woman said, placing an oversized purse on the table between them. "Is that an odd thing to say?"

"Not at all. We'd like to think it's a safe space." Lissa gestured over to the table, "We'll sit over there. Make yourself comfortable." Lissa closed the door slowly, ignoring Annika's death stare. "Tell me your full name and birthdate," Lissa said as she sat down.

"Tamara Rain Dungee. 1962. Oh, what beautiful Tarot cards."

"Thank you. They were designed over fifty years ago." Lissa shuffled. "Cut or shuffle these. Can you give me the day and time of day, if possible?"

"Oh, uh, March 13th, 4 a.m. or so."

Lissa jotted this down and smiled. Cards can be interpreted in different ways, and most tutorials will say—with a slight disclaimer—that skewing things toward the positive will get you more regular customers. But this woman's cards showed a clear trajectory. She had a confrontation coming up, and it wouldn't be pleasant. Lissa frowned.

"The Moon is about intuition and dreams. You are looking within for answers, which is good, but the answers that you seek may already have revealed themselves."

The woman nodded, eager for more.

"The Tower, in this order, suggests you may need to watch out for flying objects," Lissa said in a dry voice. She had a sharp vision of the woman being hit in the head with something heavy and blunt. Perhaps glassware or a decorative stone. Wary of claiming to be a prophet of any sort, she was hesitant to share her occasional visions with clients in case she was wrong. Annika used to get frustrated with Lissa's self-doubt, explaining that, "When we second guess, we're not trusting the magic that holds the deepest truths." Part of Lissa never wanted to have visions as intense as Annika's because they seemed burdensome, but when they came she felt cosmically obligated to share. "I mean that rather literally with you. Usually, there is symbolism. A dream of flying objects, for instance—but I think you may want to watch out a few days. I feel the force of something forthcoming. It doesn't necessarily mean you will get hit, of course. This can be symbolic for the way an event will hit you."

"He liked to throw things when he was on hallucinogens." Tammy looked down in her lap, tears welling in her eyes. "Will he ever leave me alone?"

"He doesn't want to." Lissa closed her eyes and sensed that she was wrong. She was missing something. This kid didn't want anything positive for his mother. He was hissing, *Tell her to watch her back. Tell her to try to run. She was no mother.* But how to warn her? Should she?

"I just want him to leave me alone. Forgiveness isn't an option.

He was a little shit." Anger sparked in her eyes, quickly replaced with a look of guilt. "I'm sorry; I know I'm supposed to be bigger than that, but I tried everything with that kid. What can I do?"

Lissa took her time tuning in, and she saw a clear division. "I think you've already done what you can, and now you need to change the way he sees you. Emotionally, you're indulging the fight. If you can release the need to be right, it'll be like a different existence."

The customer stood, annoyed. "Thank you. You know, I did everything I could." Her face hardened as she rolled her shoulders back with a pop. It looked as though she was about to storm out, but she stopped, reaching for one of the crystals on the counter.

"I hear you," Lissa said calmly, watching the way the woman held the crystal.

"Do I tip you? I know you tried your best. I'm not trying to be mean, but I don't like this blame the victim woo woo bullshit." She waved her hands around, as if to emphasize her point.

"No need to tip. No blame." Lissa could hear Annika sighing and the ghostly teenager hissing; *I have nothing else to do. I'm going to keep harassing her till she joins me.* "Would you like me to contact our jeweler for that, Raven?" She tipped her head towards the crystal. "I can have him call you."

"I'm sorry. I have to think about all this." Tammy said, her brows furrowed. She eyed Lissa's purse in the corner.

Lissa nodded, shrugging her shoulders and smiled slightly, looking back at the exposed pepper spray. Tammy squeezed Lissa's arm as she turned to walk out of the store. "I appreciate your guidance. I guess there's no cure-all, and I'm a bit defensive I'll admit, but I hope you understand. He's only been gone a year."

"This is deep work," Lissa said. "Many of us have deep work to do. You're very brave, and you showed up here for a reason."

An hour till her shift was over, Lissa did a clearing ritual to ensure the teenager was gone. It's only easy to banish spirits that aren't tied to a person in some way. There was no doubt the woman would be back. This was a process.

Lissa handed Annika the final tally for the day's work. Annika removed her glasses to reveal too much charcoal eyeliner. She had been rolling note-sized papers with easy candle spells into decorative scrolls while humming to a tune that Lissa couldn't place. She didn't look up.

"Those look nice, Annika." When she didn't respond, she added, "Did you hear me?"

"Yeah, I'll make the transfer at the end of the day. Glad to avoid another overdraft fee," Annika said, without looking up. She checked her phone. "Your mother messaged me twice looking for you. Good luck on your date this week." She said it genuinely, with no hint of attitude.

"Ugh. I was worried that might be what it is."

Annika looked up. "It's definitely a date." She glanced at the door. "That woman's son is hanging on, isn't he?"

Lissa nodded.

"I'll take care of him. He's a tough spirit."

"Annika, look, we need to talk. I mean, really talk, about what happened with that spell and Inga. I had good reason. I was wrong for not listening to you, but I feel like you're not being fair. We can burn the spell together. I can take it back."

Annika managed to smile and sneer at the same time. "Like I told you, there's no going back. And this isn't an isolated thing, Lissa." She shook her head in frustration. "You just don't get it—magic shouldn't be abused. You can't use it to manipulate. All these prosperity spells. It's not about control. It's about … Speaking of which, I want you to take *your* cat with you. You might not remember this, but *I'm* allergic."

"That's not my cat! It must be Raven's if it's not yours." Lissa said and waited for more. Annika was usually the one to fix things, so as she stared down at her phone Lissa knew it must be to look for his number or message him on social. Instead, Annika's cell dinged. Solitaire notification. "Fine then, whatever. We also got what I think is a pre-eviction notice." She considered reminding Annika that Trent was free and that she was having panic attacks. She could use a friend right now, but she couldn't stand begging for help. She'd been the project of so many healers at TLC after Trent, and though she had appreciated their efforts, the feeling of being worked on like some broken thing was not the kind of existence she wanted to return to.

"Look, I know you're feeling sorry for yourself, but you need to build a bridge and get over it," Annika said, the kindness returning to her eyes.

"Have a blessed day," Lissa told her, a spiritual fuck-you, before gently closing the door.

Lissa lived a few miles away, on Perry Avenue, and the walk was lovely in the afternoons, but not with a squirmy cat in her canvas bag. Ash kept sticking his head out of the top, and she worried he'd jump out. It was difficult to balance him on her right shoulder and hold her purse on the left with the taser tucked safely in the side pocket. "Please stop moving. There's potential for like, four different kinds of accidents here," she told him.

She moved the nozzle on one of the pepper sprays so that the safety was off and walked slowly with her thumb primed and eyes alert, appreciating the crisp breeze. The woman who'd caught her gaze at lunch walked toward her. She was at least a foot taller than Lissa, and when she passed, it seemed the breeze got colder in her wake. She walked as though she was cutting through the air, unafraid of anything or anyone. Briefly, she smiled at Lissa before making a sharp turn into a nameless office building. Lissa watched as the woman passed through the revolving door becoming less visible.

Ash mewed and batted at Lissa's hair as she examined her reflection in the side of the building. The windows were dark, clouded glass, and the sign out front showed the outline of an orchid. The building housed many offices, and the companies that occupied the space were forever rotating. Lissa sped-walked home, making a mental note to drop off a fresh set of business cards at the office later.

Aside from a few student loan bills and an Amazon box full of tea, there was nothing and no one waiting for Lissa, so she hung her key with the little pepper spray canister on a hook by the door before searching for a plastic container that might double for a litter box. Slipping off her shallow heels and feeling the delightful welcome of her cool hardwood floors, she exhaled as Ash made his rounds, exploring each corner of her apartment. She'd survived another day, but she felt like her allies were fading. She needed to get Annika to forgive her, to understand that Lissa would never use the spell she'd gotten a month ago. It was no good anyhow. She regretted leaving in anger earlier.

Her cell buzzed, then buzzed again. And again. *Mom.* She sighed, pulling out her phone.

Ash perched on Lissa's kitchen stool, already quite at home. "Smile," Lissa told him. Consciously ignoring the messages she knew were from her mother, she took his picture from a few different angles and emailed the images to a local pet lost and found site before sitting next to him at her kitchen counter. "We had a dog when I was little, but no cats. What do you even need? Tuna? Toys? Do you like feathers?"

He hopped up on the sink and began licking the faucet.

"Got it!" she said, grabbing a small bowl and filling it with water. "Let's not get on the counter though, okay?"

When she picked Ash up, she noticed that he was heavier than he looked, and she gently placed him down near the fridge. She looked inside to see if she had any cat-friendly foods, but there was barely anything in there, save a half-eaten cauliflower pizza and a lot of pre-mixed chai with rose water. "Grocery store it is."

Just before she left, her phone buzzed again.

Message 1: "Just consider a dress. I left one on your bed. It was on sale at Nordstrom. I couldn't help it."

Message 2: "This isn't a set-up, but his name is Cal. He's the sweetest man. If you want to chat before we meet, let me know. I'm around all night."

Message 3: "The Grandview Inn is kind of dimly lit, so keep that in mind."

Response 1: "Mom, I can't talk. I have to buy cat food and litter and whatever else cats need."

Message 3: "You got a cat?"

Annika

When Annika approached Inga's driveway, she slowed the car and took a moment to imagine herself surrounded by mirrors so that any magic Inga might try on her would ricochet. She parked at the end of the drive, and walked up to the purple door, pretending not to see the curtains part and quickly close. After knocking a few times, she heard her invitation.

"I'm watching my programs. Get your ass in here already, girl."

"I'm not a girl anymore," Annika said, taking a moment to register how much it seemed Inga had aged in five years. While she still had a full and deceptively sweet-looking face, there was a crinkling around her eyes that seemed to soften her gaze, if just a little. And unlike before, when she had streaks of gray, her hair was the color of vanilla icing, complete in a roller-set style.

"Alright, young woman, you've done your evaluation. You, by the way, look like shit. Don't wear makeup anymore?"

Annika glared, noticing the familiar soundtrack to *Designing Women.*

"What's on your mind? Need some candles? I have a bunch of prosperity towers in the back. I sell them on Amazon," Inga said, directing her gaze back to the 85" screen that she was sitting too close to.

"No. I don't want anything from you but information. What did you tell Lissa? Be specific."

"I don't remember. Look, the commercial is over." Waving her hand, she pointed to Delta Burke. "Shhh!"

"You're watching on-demand. You can pause it. What did you tell her? What spell did you give her? Just tell me, so I can fix whatever mess you made."

Inga's eyes widened, nothing but hardness left, and she smiled in her serpentine way. "You, my mentee, better watch your tone. Have a seat. I want to catch up, then I'll tell you."

Annika grabbed a quartz from her pocket and held it tightly. She leaned toward the old woman, forgetting how powerful her presence was, and immediately felt herself losing her edge. It took an enormous amount of energy not to recoil away from her.

"Want a beer?" Inga asked. "Kat will be home soon," she taunted, flashing her sinister smile again.

"Kat lives here?" Annika leveled her voice.

"Works as a mechanic down the way." Inga sniffed, "She's doing well, new girlfriend. Better girlfriend, if you ask me, but nothing magical about that one. She's a doormat."

"I hope Kat's happy." And she genuinely did.

"She's okay. I helped her get rid of the guilt you gave her, letting her beat on you like that. What's that martyr shit about anyway?"

"I couldn't hurt her. I couldn't."

"Looks like you got a scar there, by your eye. I don't remember that, unless you used to slather it with makeup. Seriously, girl," she shook her head. "I don't even recognize you without that inch of black eyeliner you used to wear."

"What else do we need to cover before you'll tell me?" Annika was eager to change the subject.

"Just gave her a death mantra. But she has to use it during a moment of conscious distraction, and that girl is neurotic as hell – I wouldn't worry about it if I were you."

"Her ex just got out of prison. She's a little neurotic because he tried to kill her. More than once. She's not always like that. We've worked together for years."

"Do tell." Inga rested her chin in her hands, patronizing her. She had a lacy throw over the back of her flower print chair, with matching flower print pillows. Everything about the house, from the framed cross-stitch hearts to the checkboard kitchen tiles, was quaint and busy and sweet, but everything about Inga was sharp lines and vitriol.

"Lissa and I run a shop, The Spirit House. You can't come inside though because I have guards. Spirit guards that will knock your old ass down at the door," Annika challenged.

"Mouthy! I love it. I do miss you, kid. You know that 'burden' you always say I gave you, honey? That's power, and I never gave anyone else that kind of power. You have something special. Don't waste it being a martyr or trying to save weak-willed women." She adjusted in her seat with a grunt of pain. Annika focused in on her old mentor and examined her eyes once more. Inga wouldn't meet her eyes.

"Are you okay?"

"Be a doll and grab me some water. The bubbly kind. In the door." She waved her hand in the direction of the kitchen.

Annika found one of Inga's bubble glass blown cups and poured a can of sparkling water in it, along with a single ice cube, just as she used to drink it. "Here." She noticed Inga's hand shaking slightly as she took it from her.

Inga gulped half the glass down and shifted again. "Think my kidneys are failing, kid. Look, just let that friend of yours learn her own lessons on her own time. I mean it." She pressed on, "You think you're here to save everyone, and that's just not the case. In fact, it might be best if you do leave before Kat gets home. I don't want you to try to fix her, too. She's here on her own journey, and you need to respect that."

Annika stood, looking Inga straight in the eyes, "I have the scars to prove it. I still love Kat. Tell her if you want. Or don't." Shrugging, she turned to leave.

"That's my girl. I'll go with the latter option." She pressed the pause button on the TV again, re-animating Delta Burke, and chuckled. "You know this woman won the Miss Florida title? I just think she's a lifelong beauty queen. What a life." Inga had always rattled off random facts about Hollywood stars that no one else paid attention to, and Annika nodded vacantly, the way she used to. "Hey, give me a kiss before you go. And take one of those prosperity candles. You have an aura of lack right now. You might need a boost for that little business of yours."

Annika started to hustle out the door, but paused, grabbing a tall green candle on the way. She held it, felt its power, then set it back down. "I think I can do this on my own." She closed the door tightly as she left.

Chaos

Thursday, October 28

When Pauline returned to the pawn shop, Lee's eyes betrayed his cool demeanor. He straightened his shirt and reshelved a ceramic tea set he'd had on the counter. As Pauline walked toward him, all hips in her wrap dress and flowered heels, she smiled. She had on bright yellow eyeglass frames with tiny white flowers to match her nails and offset the fire-engine red lipstick that she always ordered by the half-dozen.

"Got something there," Lee said, sniffing, pointing to her teeth.

"What?" Pauline looked behind her.

"Your teeth. Looks like your lipstick, unless you fought for your last meal." Lee smiled.

Remembering what it felt like to blush, Pauline traced her tongue over her teeth a few times as Lee nodded. "Thanks, I guess."

"You got it! I'm glad you came back. I would've felt a little dumb if you hadn't," he said, retrieving a beautifully decorated box. The silver paper shone in the late afternoon light, and there was even a bow on top. "I found a way to wrap it for you."

Pauline smiled again, quickly closing her lips. The truth was, she still didn't know whether or not to purchase the gun. Right after deciding she would, a story about another shooting on a community college campus arrived in her feed. Yet here she was. "Wow. I didn't expect this, Mr. Lee. You're a true gentleman after all. I am going to take the gun, but what's your return policy?"

"I try. Uh, no returns generally. But for you, um..." He glanced at his watch. "Twenty-two days."

"Interesting policy. Especially when you have no inventory, Lee," Pauline said, looking around. The metal shelves behind her held only a few old records and animal-shaped salt and pepper shakers.

"True. That sounds like a good excuse for a break. My gentle-manliness, that is—earned me a few hours over martinis and the finest microgreen salad you can imagine?"

"Did you Google that?"

"Not that one, no. I know microgreens quite intimately."

"Huh, aren't you quite the contradiction, then." She laughed, relaxing a little.

The two of them exchanged a smile that held agreement, the way old friends might, as Pauline retrieved her credit card. "You do look ready for a drink now. What are your plans? I have to be somewhere in a few hours, so I could go somewhere nearby."

"The place I was thinking is fifteen minutes away."

"Too long. We could warm up a booth at the Grandview Inn. I doubt they have your microgreens, but I can be guaranteed a good house or Caesar." She felt the forward momentum of adrenaline again and wasn't sure if it was him, the gun, the shop, or the sheer novelty of all factors combined.

By the time Pauline led Lee to the heavy wooden doors, she felt the blanket of nostalgia as the smell of salty fries with undertones of mildew wrapped around her. "Seat Yourself," a sign instructed, so she walked toward her regular booth, the very spot where she was supposed to be meeting her daughter in a few hours.

"This is nice and understated," Lee said looking around at the wood paneled walls and dark décor. "I'm surprised there's no taxidermy."

"They took it down." She added, wryly, "Probably after a complaint. The neighborhood has changed so much." Pauline took a seat and noted the lack of bounce to the booth cushion. "I honestly don't know what came over me, how we're sitting here together," she admitted. She supposed she would wait on Cal and Lissa after having a fun conversation with Lee, and that would be that. But in that case, maybe a martini wasn't the best idea.

When a twenty-something server arrived at their table, adjusting her vest as though she had just thrown it on, Lee rubbed his palms together vigorously. "Two martinis," he said. "It'll be my first one in quite a few years," he confided, leaning across the booth. "Not to pressure you."

"I'm witnessing your first martini after years?"

"You're making a prep out of me," he said. "I really am more of a tequila man."

"Put a lime in his," Pauline called after the waiter. She looked around the bar at all the empty tables and wondered if the restaurant was always so deserted now. The recession had crushed a lot of businesses, especially restaurants, and while new businesses were barreling in, all the staples were getting pushed out. She traced the crease in the gold booth cushion and tried to remember what color it was when she came here as a child, back when her family would have to wait forty-five minutes for the worst tables–right here in the bar, but on the other side, by the bathrooms.

Years later, she came here with Michael almost every weekend for date nights before he started traveling, and even then they'd have to wait on bar seating as early as 4 p.m. Now, she removed her glasses and began to rub the bridge of her nose. Maybe the seats had been a dark maroon. Or brown.

"You're not really regretting this, are you?"

"It's been a long day, Lee. It's not you."

"Tell me," Lee said. "I'm here to listen. It's a superpower of mine."

"That is rare." Pauline wasn't sure what to share exactly, or even how to organize her thoughts. She was used to asking the questions.

The server arrived, holding the stems of two martini glasses. She bent her knees slowly and, in an effort to be overly careful, psyched herself out and managed to spill both martinis just as she placed them down on the napkins. "Shoot." She looked about ready to cry.

"Thanks," Pauline said warmly, patting her hand. "No worries. Are either of the owners here today?"

"There's only one owner. He bought the place a year ago, and he's not here very often anymore. I'm sorry I spilled your drink." She retrieved a few extra napkins at the bar behind them and began to furiously wipe up the small spills.

"No, no, I'm not asking to complain, "she reassured the girl. "It's just I knew the owners, the previous ones. I thought I would say hello. I grew up coming here. Are you always this slow these days?"

The girl looked relieved. "We get busy after 6 p.m. This is early for most people to eat, I mean, most of the time. Can I get you anything else?"

"Salads!" Lee said, rubbing his hands together and smiling with overexaggerated glee.

"No, no salad. The martini's fine for me," Pauline said, placing a hand unwittingly on Lee's. "Thanks, though." His knuckles were rough, as was the skin around his nails, and she immediately wanted to pull out the moisturizer she kept in her purse and ease it into his skin.

"Guess I'll wait to make myself a nice grilled cheese at home then. I can't eat alone in front of you. That'd remove any chivalry points I've earned." Lee took a sip of his martini instead. "Holy shit! That's all vodka," he said. The server stood for an awkward moment, as though they might change their minds, then nodded and rushed off to the back of the bar to start her shift change duties, which she seemed to be referring to on a list.

"Indeed!" Pauline said. She glanced over at the young woman wiping down equipment, then refilling ice, wondering who the new owner was. This poor girl seemed to be the only person working today, dutifully dusting each of the Tiffany-style lamps that sat along the old wooden bar.

Lee cleared his throat. "So, you grew up coming here? It looks like it was fancy back in the day. Nice childhood, huh?"

"Not bad. My parents weren't perfect. They didn't have a lot, but we'd come here for birthdays—it was fancy, in a way. The restaurant used to have a sundae bar over in that corner. It was row after row of ice cream, whipped cream, frozen yogurt, the works, but they served it out of a bathtub. There was a sink full of toppings, everything from fruit to hot fudge sauce."

"That's class. The best we got as kids was the fancy McDonald's near Main Street that had the plastic play area and giant Grimace who was always smiling. Never quite understood the purpose behind his name. Did they serve the toppings out of a toilet?" He smirked.

Pauline stared at him unsmiling. "No." She took a deep sip of the martini, draining half the glass, then sighed. "You're a little awkward, Lee, and I've never seen anyone with drier hands, but this is nice. You know, to be out."

"Day drinking is nice, or being with me?"

"A little of both." She denied herself a laugh, keeping her lips pursed. "I haven't been on a date in a long time, and it feels good. I've been walking around with a lot of guilt these last few years, and I haven't really let myself have anything good, you know? I mean, except fashion."

"You're just about perfect in that regard."

"Just about?"

"Also, I don't have that guilt problem," Lee said as he shifted on the booth. Assuming a gruff whisper, he leaned in. "I'm not as awkward as you think. I'm just nervous because I like you, and you intimidate me a little. Also, this booth is a little lopsided," he added, conspiratorially.

"You just have to find your spot," Pauline said. "So, let's be honest here. You weren't going to ask me out that day we met, were you?"

"Sure wasn't, but only because I figured I wouldn't have a shot. You look like you have a silver spoon stuck up your ass, and I look like I just got out of prison behind that pawn shop counter unshaved. Neither's true, but you know; people go by appearances." He looked down at his hands, examining them. "Do you have any lotion?"

Pauline eagerly handed him a sample sized bottle she pulled from her purse, saying, "People aren't ever as simple as we'd like them to be, are they?"

He smelled the lotion and squirted a dollop of it in the palm of his hand. "Same emotions, same bodily functions, but the rest of it is as complex at the universe. We just look simple," Lee said with a hint of whimsy, rubbing his hands together vigorously. "Tell me what you think of me truly—or, what you thought of me that day?"

"Rough around the edges is a good way to put it," she sat back, as if to assess him. "But you have something behind that. A story."

"See? You're magical." He clapped his hands.

"I don't like that word, magic. I'm logical. And I profile everyone because I've studied the social sciences. The hard part is not diagnosing. Did you go to college, Lee?"

"Started to. Philosophy. But I graduated culinary school first, then went the traditional route a little late. B-school. I was on a scholarship, night classes," he said.

"Tell me more."

"I dropped out then, too, because it felt like a racket. I didn't need it—I was an entrepreneur at heart and knew the best lesson was just to get out there and fail, then figure out why. Also, I was in love. I had two businesses before the pawn shop—a café and a bakery, and another restaurant in the works. Of course, I prioritized them, not my wife at the time."

"Whoa! Okay," she said. "You did catch me off guard with all that. So, divorcee? I'm sorry to hear. What did your wife do?"

"Baker."

"Tell me about the businesses. I always wished I had that drive." Pauline noticed the way his gaze shifted into determination when he started discussing business. He, too, had regret, he explained, as he recounted working ridiculously long hours. But it didn't seem to torture him.

"I bought the pawn shop out of the blue—get it?"

"So you just buy up whatever catches your eye?" She rolled her eyes at him. "Must be nice."

"It was a lucky break. I think, anyway. I'm beginning to wonder. The previous owner died, and the place was up for auction with everything in it. If the right people had known about it, I would've been outbid, but the family wanted to sell fast. I'm helping the ex-owner's brother sell down the inventory—that was his negotiation. He knew there were spoils in that shop, but he didn't know how to move them. Hoping to have it cleared out in under a month. I was planning to turn it into a breakfast and brunch spot after I got rid of the inventory. It was a restaurant before the pandemic hit and the building was so cheap. It seemed simpler to try to sell as much of it as possible rather than to make him an offer and have to get rid of it some other way."

"And that brings you to being a gun salesman who doesn't know anything about guns?"

"Not a big gun guy, no. I don't know about half the shit in that place. Thank God for the internet."

"You don't know anything about guns, and yet you're legally allowed to sell them?" Pauline asked, incredulously.

"Just need to be legally allowed to own them. The barrier to entry is low," he said dryly. "Don't you watch the news?"

"True. But wait a minute—you're a chef?"

"A cook, and a baker."

"Huh! Talk about emotions. What am I feeling now?" She challenged, looking around the restaurant, as though an answer might materialize in the stained-glass windows. She thought about the wheel of eight primary emotions, that she used as the starting point for some of her clients, to help them pinpoint what they felt before they dug into the nuance.

"Shock and awe is what your feeling at the moment." Lee laughed. "What other emotions are you feeling?" he asked, leaning in, his subtle forearm muscles showing.

"You're right. I think it's a surprise. In a good way. But I have so many questions. You covered a lot of ground."

"Questions are okay. I'm an open book." He opened his hands out to her, as if to demonstrate. "Shoot."

"A chef who doesn't drink martinis?" she asked, raising an eyebrow at him.

"A cook who didn't drink martinis, till today."

"Shock and awe indeed." Pauline felt her shoulders soften, and she wasn't sure if it was ease of conversation or the vodka kicking in. She wanted to tease him more—it was the most fun she'd had in years—but something else washed over her. Perhaps it was the simple realization that she had another mission tonight. They'd been sitting there for a while, and the garish wooden clock on the wall showed only an hour and a half till she was supposed to be here again to introduce Lissa and Cal. The thought of Lissa brought her back.

"Your turn," Lee said. "Tell me more about Pauline."

"My book isn't that interesting. It's all emotion. Like I was saying, guilt is the most prevalent emotion in my world right now, Lee, if I'm being honest, and maybe a little boredom. The root of guilt is shame, and it's all-consuming. Though you are awe inspiring, you are sitting with a boring retiree who was a questionable mother."

"Guilt is a motherfucker."

"Tell me about it. Settles in the gut like bad meat. I've never felt more guilty than as a mother."

"You seem like a vigilant mother to me," he said.

"Not always."

"I doubt that."

"Not when my daughter was in that hospital bed, hooked up to tubes and machines …" She stopped. "Sorry. This isn't the place."

"Go on. It's fine."

"She was there because I didn't have the courage to speak up more." Pauline looked directly up toward the ceiling, a trick for warding off tears. Noticing the yellowing gypsum board, she distracted herself by imagining what she'd do to rehab this place, beginning with opening up those ceilings around the bar.

"Somehow I'm guessing you spoke up in your own way. Kids don't listen, especially not adult kids," Lee said, pulling her gaze back. "Not that I have any."

"I drove into their wedding cake—so I'm proud of that— but it didn't make a difference. Whatever I did, it wasn't enough. I should've stopped it, even if she hated me. It would've been worth it. I should've been relentless." She looked up again, straining her eyes.

"Wait a minute here. You drove into a wedding cake?"

When all Pauline could do was shrug, Lee added, "As a baker,

I find that mildly offensive." When she didn't smile, he lowered his voice and added, "Don't blame yourself for that guy. If I blamed myself for all the shitty people who came into my life, or the people who hurt me and my loved ones, I'd be a basket case. We'd all be basket cases." He gestured his hands wildly. "Look, it sounds like your daughter is a fighter. She found a way to survive, and that's what you should take credit for. That guy was weak and tried to share his weakness with her. She didn't let him."

"Weak indeed. He sure was. And thanks, that's generous of you to say. But he's a sociopath. Clinically. He won't stop. He's out of prison now, and if I know him at all, I know he'll have a grudge that won't go away. I've got this feeling … this guilt is not just about the past. It's about now."

"Do you really think you know him?" Lee asked, eyebrows up.

"I know his type. Too well. I was a psychotherapist for years. I worked with more than a few people who were victims of his type."

"Psychotherapist, huh. That makes sense."

"Yes, and I was good. You learn to read people and understand motivations."

"Paulie, listen," he started. "You're doing all you can. You know, I'm selling this inventory to get rid of it, but a gun isn't always the best answer. I had a friend in college who was shot by accident," Lee said in a faint voice. "I know I just sold it to you, but I think a lot of times they're more trouble than they're worth."

"The more you know," Pauline said, then raised her eyebrows. "Wait, did you just call me Paulie?"

"People keep trying to come in and sell things, even though I have all those signs posted, and we got a stun gun the other day. I can trade it out, give you a refund."

Pauline was stuck on the nickname he'd just given her, which was embarrassing. It felt… Juvenile. She tried to absorb everything else he'd said. Lost a friend to gun violence. Not a fan of guns. Well, neither was she. Was he judging her for buying the gun? She wanted to respond to everything but couldn't. "I'm sorry about your friend," she said finally.

"Let's talk about ourselves again," Lee said, pushing her lotion back to her and holding out his hands as though they were freshly manicured.

"Need help with that martini, Lee?"

"No, I got it," he said defensively. He took a generous drink.

"Why don't you tell me more about your story? You're the big mystery here."

"I'll tell you in a minute. Have to drain the snake. I'm not used to this fancy day drinking like you posh people."

"Really?" Pauline said. "Did you really just say 'Drain the snake'?"

Lee laughed. "Teach me your refined ways, will you?" As he stood, Pauline noticed that he had a sort of rugged handsomeness to him, like a well-worn George Clooney. He walked with loose arms, confidence but not dominance. A baker? She tried to profile him. Maybe he'd been a nerdy kid in high school with a rough upbringing that gave him empathy. A bad relationship he invested too many years into before it exploded. Or maybe he was the kid on the block who got into trouble, but he'd had an accident or lost a friend and spent the rest of his young adulthood trying to make up his failings to his parents, then watched over them as they aged, even to the detriment of his expansion. Or maybe—

"Ma'am, would you like another martini?" the server asked. Her blonde ponytail was falling out, and Pauline wanted to fix it for her. The girl would look so nice if she swept it up into a bun.

"Um." A second martini usually led to trouble. A third led to all-out chaos. She glanced at the clock again—it was just before 3 p.m.

"Love your glasses, by the way," the server added.

Pauline smiled at her, reading the name tag. "Thank you, Sydney. Sure, why not? We'll take another round. But can you bring the check?" She reached for her phone to text Lissa.

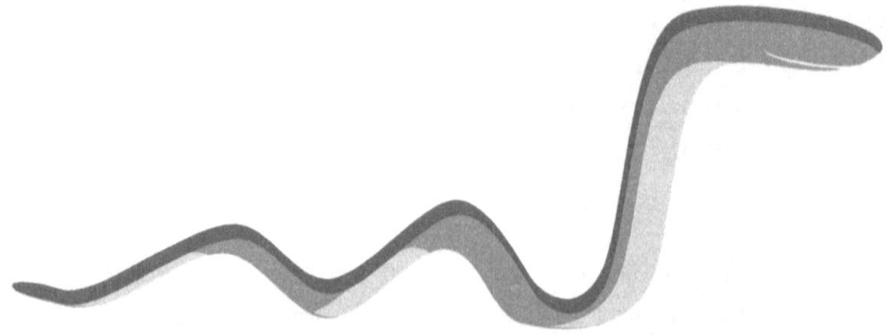

Lissa

Thursday, October 28 (4:00 p.m.)

Message 1: "I can't wait to see you soon. He can't wait either. He didn't say anything, but I know he's excited. Can you get a ride? Put it on my card."

Message 2: "Don't order the salmon. I know it's healthy, but fish is fish. You don't want to smell like the sea if he leans in to tell you a joke. You know what I mean?"

Message 3: "You are taking a bit step here. I'm proud of you. I'll leave if you hit it off."

Message 4: "Big step, not bit. Damn autocorrect."

Response 1: "I'll see you there, Mom."

Video: "I'm proud of you, kid," Pauline said with a slight slur. Lissa played it again, trying to figure out where her mother was and why she seemed drunk. Another text came in promptly, this time from Annika.

"You left your litterbox. Or 'cat box' as you call it."

"I couldn't walk home with a litterbox, fucking hell," Lissa wrote, but before she sent the text, she paused. Annika had been her mentor, and she really was allergic to cats. The litter box was probably irritating her. Lissa could vaguely remember them talking about how allergic she was sometime that spring, when they were still friends, after Lissa asked why Annika didn't have any pets. She deleted the draft and wrote: "We need to talk sooner than later. The cat is NOT mine. I took it to be nice and am waiting for Raven to respond. Pls throw the litter away. The box might be his."

Raven, a nomad, was a talented ceramic artist and jewelry maker who worked part-time for TSH, but he was also a wildcard who couldn't be put on any kind of regular schedule. For over a month last year, he'd set up shop in the wooded area behind the office building, because he said indoor spaces had become too claustrophobic. Back then, he worked almost daily and was a wonder with clients. Sales went up 25% when he was around. But Annika and Lissa later found out that he had a sleeping bag tucked behind the pines for an entire moon cycle. While he didn't leave much evidence, one sighting of him from O'Malley and she would kick them out.

Shortly after Annika confronted him, he disappeared for an entire season, taking spring to hike the Tetons and soul search. He said that he understood their fear but couldn't respect it. "True freedom lies within. You can't wait for the world's approval." Raven was twenty-seven, and Lissa imagined his parents, who lived in a million-dollar beach house somewhere in East Hampton, still gave him an allowance.

His worn shoes and slightly greasy hair portrayed an image of poverty at odds with his ability to travel the world on a whim and indulge his spiritual quests. The only correspondence they had from him included cryptic messages like "The body climbs the mountain as the soul dances with the rocks."

It'd be easy to imagine Raven letting a cat in the shop, but what Lissa couldn't imagine was Raven going through the trouble of getting the cat a collar and tag. After leaving him a third inquiry, Lissa placed her phone on the counter and glanced out the kitchen window at her cozy neighborhood. Would Trent leave a cat as a message? He'd always teased her about her superstitions. Would he plant this cutie in her shop to mess with her mind?

"I'm paranoid," she said, and her phone lit up and buzzed, as though searching for a remedy, even though Lissa had removed the RoboHealth app. The app would listen to everything and use every health-oriented data point in its assessments and recommendations. People believed it better than doctors saying it was more "holistic" and better than therapists because it saw a person navigating various moods. "Speaking of paranoia ..."

She turned off the phone.

Trent had once seemed like a genuinely good person. Smart, handsome, endearing, and full of surprises. He was exceptionally close to his family, especially his mother, who liked to brag about how poor her family had been, moving from Appalachia before her husband's landscaping business took off.

Trent would regularly hide gifts and love letters around the house for Lissa. When he figured out that she couldn't care less about jewelry and shoes, he offered more generous gifts that better understood her. He'd given her a trip to Mexico on her thirtieth birthday, a weekend yoga retreat, and even a new hybrid car when her old junker got a third recall notice. She'd watched with admiration as he sustained his family's company, which he'd built from a mildly successful small business to a multi-county enterprise with a staff of thirty. So many people had started small businesses since the government's incentive program, but so few found success. The man was no dummy. At least, not till he lost his temper.

In retrospect, she'd seen him act in a calculating way only a few times in the first few years. Once, when he suspected an employee was stealing by encouraging customers to pay in cash, he let it continue purposefully, until he had enough evidence to press charges and ruin the guy's life. Lissa had mentioned that it seemed more decent to just fire or discipline him, but Trent wanted revenge. Not knowing anything about the way the prison system worked, Lissa wondered if that guy was in there with him now. After years in prison, who wouldn't have the patience for psychological warfare?

Since he'd been released, Trent had regularly updated his social media pages. The dormant business page lit up with a "We're Back!" message, to great fanfare. The post included an image of him grinning in a white button-up with "Green Lawns Ohio" inscribed in green next to a cartoon oak tree. In the image, he looked like the loveliest man in the world—like the guy she'd originally met at a café, who had handed her a napkin after she spilled a caramel latte all over her silk blouse on the way to work.

She knew it wasn't healthy to internet stalk him now. From a spiritual standpoint, she was feeding his energy and allowing him to take up more space in her life—but it was a comfort to see him check in at local restaurants two states away.

She sat down on the bed and imagined a different reality, one in which she'd never met Trent, never given up her job or her dreams to help him as he went to night school for business. Then again, that life didn't seem like hers to fantasize about anymore. She knew too much now, and she was giving back in other ways. But if only she could just live, not worry about night terrors and panic attacks or, worse, someone seeking revenge. The smiling professional on that social post contained the threat of losing her breath.

Lissa assessed the too-small flower-print dress her mother had left her a few days ago. It hung in her closet amongst her monochrome outfits, situated by color and shade. She felt the temptation of curling up in bed and watching the Weather Channel with Ash nestled in her lap, but instead she got up and reached for her oversized top and jeans, then thought again and grabbed her favorite jeans before jumping in the shower.

Just as she was heading out the door, Lissa powered on her cell, and it buzzed again. Her Uber.

"Watch the house, Ash," she called. Ash, who was curled up near the couch, blinked his eyes open only briefly before settling back into sleep. Part of her was glad no one had claimed him yet. She scratched the top of his head, finding a moment of tenderness. "Sleep well."

In the back seat of an old Jeep, headed to a dinner that she imagined would be awkward to the point of absurdity, Lissa glanced at her phone. It was 4:32 p.m., and she was twenty minutes away, so she'd be early. Her cell buzzed again. The same number had called her three times now, and the area code, 260, traced to Portland, Indiana, where Trent's mother lived. It could be a robocaller that had picked up on her recent search history. But what if it wasn't? Lissa's panic returned. She wished her magic were stronger, more commanding, like Annika's.

The twenty-something driver wore a ballcap and glasses, and prattled on about the weather forecast, something about a basketball game, and finally how this was only his third week on the job since he'd gotten his license back. "Since the pandemic aftershock, these places needed to hire people like crazy. I got a job at three different car services, and I barely sleep I work so much."

"Comforting," Lissa muttered, Googling the phone number.

"Yeah," he carried on, "I think I'll pay off my student loans in no time at this rate. I only had to take out a few thousand anyway. I got a scholarship. First gen."

"Congratulations." Lissa wondered why she hadn't heard from her mother. She had expected at least ten more texts by now. And what was with the slurring? If nothing else, maybe the strangeness of this night would distract her from her fears.

"So, what do you study?" Lissa asked the driver after a beat. Before he had a chance to answer, Lissa noticed a Mercedes truck quickly cutting into their lane in front of them. "Hey, I don't think that driver sees you," she started to say, wondering briefly if it was Trent. The driver wasn't visible.

The Uber driver veered over, trying to avoid the collision, and in a rush of color and horns, Lissa felt time speed up, then coming to a sudden stop as the front end of the Jeep landed on the median strip. There was a scraping sound from underneath the car as the front wheel perched on the step of concrete. Horns honked and faded as Lissa's body was propelled forward, then back, forward, then back. She felt the impact of her head against the driver's side seat before her body went limp and fell sideways, draped over the backseat. Everything went still and silent, except a corner of Lissa's mind that told her to pay attention. Through clouded eyes, she could see the driver slumped over the steering wheel, dazed.

In the darkness, Trent arrived. His eyes took in everything, and all she could see was his face, twisted by anger. His knife's glint became a flash of light, and she heard her own voice in the distance.

"I'll kill you if you touch me," she heard herself yell.

"You'll what?" She felt the tear of skin breaking under the blade, his bodyweight heavy on her. He laughed then, before slicing her delicate skin, as though it was just another thing for him to do, a necessary chore: deliberate and calculated. He sliced into her again, and for a split second it was painful enough that Lissa wished he'd just finish the job so she wasn't where she was today—barely able to function in the world.

When she reoriented, she realized that this was her chance. As her body came to life beneath her, she knew she had a decision to make. Lissa could hear the driver's voice piercing into her consciousness, and she knew her window of opportunity would close as fast as it opened. She began a low chant, and she pictured her ex-husband coming at her. Only this time, she was ready. She wrapped him in black light and visualized him losing strength, losing breath. She continued the chant: heart slowing, slowing, slowing and stop. Encircling you in darkness, I see your heart slowing, slowing, slowing, and coming to a stop.

She continued the chant until the world around her steadied. Feeling the shakiness ease, Lissa could make out a sliver of light, but still felt her eyelids weighed down by gravity.

"Can you hear me? Ma'am?" The driver's young voice cracked. "Are you speaking in tongues?"

It took all Lissa's strength to blink her eyes open, to escape the nightmare, but when she did, the driver's worried eyes greeted her. She let the light in and registered his panicked expression, the creasing between his brows.

"Are we okay?" she asked.

"I was going to ask you that. I didn't know what to do. Can you sit up? Should I call an ambulance, or take you to a doctor? We had to get off the road, but I was able to stop the car safely. I think you hit your head."

Lissa sat up straighter and took a deep breath. "I think I'm okay," she said. "How long have I been out? Did you see the driver?"

"Some woman. I got the license plate, but she took off. I'm gonna sue."

"Are you sure it was a woman?"

"Are you sure you're okay?" the kid asked again, tilting his head. "You weren't out for long. Like a few minutes, but you were making some crazy sounds Can you sit up?"

"I'm good. Fine." Sitting up, she tried to shake off the dizziness. "I hope the spell doesn't work ... No, no way it worked."

"I don't understand," the driver said.

"Just drop me on the corner." Lissa tried to direct her breath to her lower belly. Once again, she glanced down at her phone. No new calls. Her phone had navigated to a link to buy First Aid supplies.

Lissa saw the restaurant up ahead, but she couldn't imagine following through with this dinner date. She hadn't dated anyone since leaving Trent, and she couldn't imagine being attracted to another person, let alone stomaching a man her mother had chosen. And now she had an excuse. She could easily text her mother and say she was traumatized, then head home to watch the Weather Channel and eat a bowl of Cheerios. Mom would understand—but then Lissa would be alone in her apartment with her new cat, terrified.

"Here we are, the Grandview Inn. If I wasn't working, I'd ask to join you for a happy hour drink, but I think I'm going to park and walk a bit. Walking clears my head. I might call my mom," he said.

"That's a good idea. Definitely call your mom. You'll be okay—you'll just have to up your insurance payment."

"Sorry again, ma'am. Whew! What a week. You look okay, but are you sure you're okay? I can take you to the hospital. Or home. I wasn't trying to ..."

Lissa cracked her neck and felt a surge of energy pool at the base of her skull. Everything became clearer in that instant. "No. The restaurant is fine."

"Gotcha."

Maybe because she had zero expectations, Lissa was hardly surprised when, now twenty minutes late as opposed to early, she still beat her mother and this supposedly perfect man to the restaurant. Pauline liked to make an entrance, no matter the situation or appropriateness. Lissa still remembered her mother's dramatic arrival to her wedding, just after the ceremony began; the aisle had been walked and Lissa stood next Trent, who she genuinely loved at the time, when Pauline drove right into the cake display while blasting Joan Jett. She was late to everything—and not just five or ten minutes late like Annika. If Pauline was a half-hour late, it was a good day. It was her power move. And as a psychologist, she had to know what she was doing.

The Grandview Inn wasn't exactly a fancy choice, but it was nice enough, a family restaurant Lissa remembered going to as a kid. Rustic chandeliers hung low in the center of the dining room and a row of booths sat against the walls near the bar. A balding man with round glasses who was dressed in a suit jacket smiled at her, and she smiled back. She began to walk toward him when another man pushed past her and took the seat across from him. They held hands.

Circling back to a slight blond server, who was giving her a side glance, Lissa asked for the table and was shown back to a small, private booth nestled next to the bathrooms.

"Can we have a table in the center of the room, or over there?" she asked, pointing to something more central, less intimate.

"You want to change the reservation?" The girl looked around the nearly empty restaurant.

"Yes. Party of three."

"Well, we're slow today, but I need to check." Lissa nodded, empathetic, as the server placed three menus down. "Can I get you anything to drink?"

"Sauvignon Blanc. Anything from New Zealand."

The woman just stared at her blankly.

"Or California. Or White Zin?"

"We have California."

Lissa took the seat closest to the bathroom where she had a good vantage point of the front door so she could watch people come in. And watch she did. She watched for what seemed years, realizing that she hadn't looked at her phone since arriving. As a server came over to ask if she wanted another glass of wine, the first of which Lissa had downed in three gulps, she powered on her phone and saw fourteen messages.

"No thank you, but my party should be here soon." She began to scroll.

Messages 1-14: (in a nutshell): "Not going to be there. Sorry. It's been an odd day, but I have to help someone out."

Response 1: "It's okay, Mom." Sensing a set-up, but giving her mother the benefit of the doubt, she added, "An old patient? I understand."

Message 15: "I told Cal something came up last minute, but he hasn't responded. Is he there?"

"Is this a setup, to get us alone?" Lissa typed, but she didn't send it. She didn't have the energy to fight, even over text. It was probably one of her mother's old clients. A suicide attempt or something. Probably not, but maybe. She gave her the benefit of doubt.

"Can I get you anything else?" a server, appearing out of nowhere, asked.

"No. Have you seen a guy about my age come in?"

The server shrugged. "What you see is what you get." The restaurant was almost empty except for the two men who were leaving their booth and a few of waitstaff on break.

"I think I'll place an order to go. Number 14 on the menu. And fries—they smell good."

"It'll be about fifteen minutes."

Lissa walked along the back of the bar and toward a two-stall bathroom painted dark blue, almost black. Not your typical restaurant bathroom color. This place used to scare her as a child because it was so dark, and full of mounted animal heads. She was glad at least that had changed. She stared at the silver door and wondered what was going on. She did feel off. Shock maybe. A part of her was relieved, glad to go home. She wasn't sure she could take her mother and this Dr. Gregory guy's company right now anyway.

Just as she approached the sink, a wave of frigid air entered the bathroom, and Lissa teetered, as though on a boat. As she struggled to steady herself, she heard her own voice chanting, and was thrust against the sink. A bottle of hand soap was knocked off the edge and rolled past her on the tiled floor.

"What the—" The rocking stopped, and Lissa wondered if this was some new version of a panic attack, or something more serious. She'd only been practicing magic for five years, a drop in the bucket, and she wasn't sure what to do. Was she losing her mind? Was she still in the restaurant? Were there earthquakes in Ohio now? Was she having an aneurysm? She noticed the glass mirror was cracked down the middle and examined the two halves of her face closely.

"The right side is what the world sees. The left side is who you truly are," Annika had told her when they were still residents at TLC.

Lissa stared at the two women in the mirror, the two sides of herself, not convinced that either was who she truly was. She stared till her vision went blurry, as though scrying with her own reflection. It moved and danced like fire, and she had to steady herself, placing her hands down and leaning onto the sink. After a time, the door opened, and an elderly lady looked at her with concern in her eyes as she said hello on her way to the stall. Lissa noticed the woman's face shift to Inga's. She stepped back then, realizing the spell had worked.

Back at the booth, Lissa picked up her Caesar salad with salmon and fries and carried it outside, passing a Tesla as it parked out front. She reached in her purse, past the pepper spray and taser, and instead grabbed some all-natural lip tint that she applied sparingly as she walked to the corner. Her eyes were jumpy; she could feel them twitching. She couldn't live this way—lighting sage and letting her life fall apart—and there was no way that recitation in an Uber had done anything.

The bus added a half hour to the journey, and as Lissa sat staring out the window to the sounds of snoring and of rap music escaping from someone's headphones, she couldn't shake the feeling that some part of her had broken. She recalled the crash, the forward momentum and vision of Trent, the desire to do anything to keep him away. She replayed the scene until the bus dropped her off near a café two blocks from home. She speed-walked with her carryout, eager to hide away from the world. When she got home, a sudden wave of exhaustion hit, and she fell into a deep sleep on the couch. Her salad and fries remained on the counter, and her front door remained unlocked. She awoke to an almost dead cellphone. Ash was curled up in the corner watching her. "How long did we sleep?" she asked him. His tail twitched in response as he jumped off the couch.

He rushed to the fridge, which was where she'd previously fed him, so Lissa eased herself up and toward the food dish to acquiesce. "To be honest buddy, I just want to go back to sleep."

Ash started eating before Lissa had the chance to fully place the food bowl down. "Geesh!"

Noticing the door had been left unlocked, she felt a surge through her chest and rushed to lock it, then went to charge her phone in the bedroom. She saw a text from Annika, as she did every Friday, which showed the shop numbers for the week. Things looked bad.

"I don't think I'll be in today. I'm not feeling well," Lissa wrote the next day.

She watched as Annika started to write a text back. It showed she was typing, then stopped. Typing, then stopped. Finally, a message came in that simply said, "I know. You missed your shift. Are you okay?"

Lissa looked around. "Oh, sorry. Got into a car accident yesterday. I'm fine, just shaken up."

"Sure you're okay?"

"Yeah." It was nice that she was expressing concern.

"Well, things are fine here. Raven showed up last night, so no worries about not coming in. I already put him to work. He says it's not his cat, by the way."

"???" Lissa wrote. She waited for Annika to say something else, but nothing came in, so she pulled up Trent's Facebook page. Ash rushed in and hopped up on the bed, curling up near her and purring.

"Hey, cutie. I'm starting to hope no one comes looking for you, Ash," she told the cat, and he mewed. She almost turned her phone off without looking. But as though someone else lifted her hand, she unlocked it again. On Facebook, the artificially kind-faced man, the fake Trent, who stared back at her now—the man she'd kissed and promised herself for eternity to, who'd tried to kill her more than once—was surrounded in pink. Someone had put a frame around him and a soft filter. It looked like he'd been made into an angel. She scrolled down and found a brief post written by his mother.

"To all the people who loved my boy Trent, it is with a heavy heart that I inform you that he passed away suddenly a few hours ago. We thank you for your prayers and wishes. –Lena"

The world turned gray, panic rose in her throat as she read and reread the message, trying not to feel so terrible about the relief she felt. Had she done this? Could it be a coincidence? She shook her head in confusion, as if somehow that would bring her clarity. She wasn't that powerful, and she wasn't even sure she'd remembered the chant right. Half the magic she did wasn't literal. It was symbolic now, a way to navigate the world—right? But even asking herself this question felt disingenuous.

She recalled the chant she'd been given, the simple spell that could slow a feeling, a habit, or, if used as intended, a person's heart. She stared at her ex-husband's cherubic face, filtered and disguised, and she could see his anger simmering beneath the smile that never reached his eyes.

"Did I kill you?" she asked the image.

As she opened another tab and began searching for more information about Trent, she heard the scraping of keys, her heart skipping a beat. She reopened the tab and, not knowing what else to do, blocked his account. She rushed to light a protective candle and begin to cast a circle. During her ritual, the heaviness returned, compressing her organs, and constricting her breath. "Get off of me," she yelled, and the pressure intensified. He might've been dead, but Trent was here.

She needed help. She needed to know what was happening.

When in TLC with Annika, Lissa had learned about remote viewing. She tried to remember what her friend had told her, how a witch can stay on the physical plane and travel out of her body to view others in real time. She needed to know what was happening, and with every ounce of energy she had, she summoned the ability to move her energy elsewhere. When she closed her eyes and focused on Pauline, she found herself in the office of another psychologist.

Cal

Lissa's eyes fluttered open, her current surroundings fading into a new reality. Suddenly, the energy of Trent became weaker, and she found herself in an office with gray walls and white trim. She looked down at her hands. They still looked like her hands, but she felt different, lighter. Looking around the room, Lissa could see Cal clearly. His sensitive gaze and kind eyes.

She remembered Annika's advice for remote viewing: "Don't get involved. You can only watch, but you can decide when and even go into the past." So, she focused on Cal, when they were supposed to meet. Cal wrote down the date and time and a few notes from his last session. He'd just excused a client and was pacing the office. It felt like a movie to Lissa at first, and she tried to focus harder, to zoom in. As she got closer to this man, she felt his loneliness and confusion.

Thursday, October 28 (4:00 p.m.)

Cal couldn't settle down, and he couldn't shake the feeling that he was being watched. His last client was gone, but it felt like she was still there. She'd complained about her unhappy marriage for an hour, which Cal empathized with but—if he was being entirely honest—his true thoughts were on himself. He never understood why he hadn't found a wife. He just couldn't seem to find anyone interested in him on his own. Sure, mothers always loved him, but what did that matter if their daughters didn't?

Lissa would probably be the same. Maybe he was too safe and too boring. This would make sense since the maternal gaze focused on security and steadiness, which, Cal had to admit, he was ready to offer. And to call him boring wasn't fair exactly, he just liked routine. And work. To deviate from this was never good.

He wanted nothing more than to find a decent human being to settle down with. Someone he could adore. Someone he could talk with about news and work over long dinners or brunches on the weekends, and who'd challenge him intellectually, who'd share with him what she was passionate about. Someone who was as spirited as Renee, his ex, only less narcissistic. Less like a bottomless, boundless hole that could never be filled. Not that he was bitter, or anything.

Not usually one to stereotype, for self-preservation reasons Cal had sworn off professional artists. It wasn't that he disliked them. At one time, he'd wanted to be one himself, but he only spent fifteen credits in undergrad studying art history and experimenting with acrylic paints and oils before he realized that artists were so good at seeing the world anew because they refused to look at the same thing twice. For a routine-driven man, traveling the world sounded more like a sentence than a dream.

Nonetheless, he still had fond memories of growing up watching Bob Ross with his parents. When *The Joy of Painting* was on, the constant pressure between them had been off. No glasses were being thrown after one too many martinis. No heated make-out sessions *right in front of the kids* because they couldn't keep their hands off each other. The family was mesmerized by Ross, his voice like a tonic, neutralizing Cal's parents.

When Cal graduated from college, he realized he wanted to help people find steadiness and equilibrium. He felt called to do so—almost as though he didn't have a choice. A small part of him still wanted to do something with a more predictable outcome. Of course, his mother and father had been insistent he specialize, and, to keep up with his over-achieving pediatrician brother, Cal took the road most followed. And he didn't regret it. Meanwhile, specializing felt limiting.

He always suspected the best way to treat a person was to find a unique formula that allowed greater clarity. After all Cal's years of study, and two graduate degrees with some of the finest psychologists on the planet, he still felt this way. Everyone's story was nuanced and unique, a formula so complex that the best a psychologist could hope for were honest answers and enough information to point someone in the right direction. All treatment, when it came to the mind, was self-directed. Even when it came to medications. This is when he started working on the RoboHealth app. He didn't love the name, and he understood why some people were wary, but the technology had the potential to do what no one else could, he thought. It could solve the mystery of the individual, across conditions, through constant monitoring.

He'd had the idea after a client called him with a suicide threat. It had occurred four times throughout his career, and today was the fourth. He was supposed to be meeting Pauline and her daughter, but when he saw the number appear on his phone, the entire world fell away. Though he knew recovery would ultimately be up to the patient, he had to do all he could. He sat on the phone for an hour with Mrs. Jonson, who said that since her husband died, she'd have intermittent thoughts of drinking a glass of bleach or taking all the pills he'd left behind in the cupboards.

"I can't seem to throw them away," she explained. "I haven't tried anything, but . . ." Cal sat and listened. He told her it was okay to cry. He told her more help was on the way, using his private line to put in a request. He listened and spoke gently, offered all the resources he could, and when the client seemed calm and he'd verified that more help was on the way, he hung up and got in his car to head over to his dinner. Half-way there, Mrs. Jonson called back just to thank him, but she didn't seem to want to get off the phone.

He was just wrapping up the call. Mrs. Jonson apologized for interrupting what she knew must be his "wonderfully busy" life and promising that she would be okay and the medics had arrived at her house, but she just wanted to let him know how much his time meant. Cal appreciated the gesture and was glad to hear Mrs. Jonson's voice clarify, but just as he hung up again, he saw the woman with wavy dark hair leaving The Grandview Inn. He was sure it was Lissa, and he fought the urge to duck when she glanced over at his Tesla. Cal's windows were tinted, so though he could see her clearly, she couldn't see him, but he always forgot this.

It was definitely her. He remembered the picture of Lissa in a simple gray top and jeans that sat on Pauline's desk when he had first started. In the image, she was staring into the camera as though it might offer her the answers she desired. Her face was slightly angular, boasting high cheekbones, with deep-set eyes that penetrated, and she had a subtle scar along one side of her face that didn't detract from her radiance.

Cal was transfixed by that photo. He wondered about the scar, but never asked. Feeling his phone vibrate, he sighed, expecting to see Mrs. Jonson's number again.

Instead, it buzzed and dinged a few times in a row, and he saw a series of messages from Pauline he'd missed while he was on the phone with Mrs. Jonson. She'd called off the dinner for some reason. Feeling badly as she'd been stood up twice in one day now, he debated a moment over whether to chase Lissa down and offer her a ride.

Ultimately, he decided that might seem creepy. He'd wait for a more appropriate time to meet. Nonetheless, he felt regret nudging him as he drove past her at the bus stop. She looked shaken, and, like always, he wanted to help. He waited there until he saw the bus and followed it home to make sure she got there safely. But when she looked back and caught his gaze through the window, he felt something in him seize. The only way he could explain it to himself later was that it was otherworldly, as though Lissa were a ghost but not really, as though she were walking between worlds.

All time seemed to stop, and Cal found himself unable to drive. He felt shaken, almost as though he'd just been in an accident, and he didn't feel alone. There was a feeling of being watched or followed. He pulled over and hobbled inside the nearest restaurant and did something he never did—he ordered a gin and tonic and sat at the bar alone, trying to collect his thoughts.

Pauline

T hursday, October 28 (4:15 p.m.),
"You have a nice place," Pauline said, genuinely surprised. They entered through the back door to a large kitchen with a center island and dozens of pots and pans hanging overhead. There was a long dining table adorned with simple gray placemats, as though primed for a dinner party. Beyond the kitchen, Pauline could see a cozy living room with no television and a small bookshelf with thick, genre novels, mostly Stephen King, lining the shelves. "I can't believe you live two blocks from the Grandview Inn, a chef, and you've never been there."

"Cook and baker. This is where I do my best work," Lee said.

"Well thanks for letting me sober up here. I have less than an hour. I can't believe we had two martinis before 4 p.m.," Pauline said. "I should probably head back to the restaurant by quarter till. Do you have any coffee? I don't plan on eating there. I just want to introduce the kids and duck out. Maybe it'd be better if I never showed up. Then they'd be forced to talk. They're both a little shy."

"Seems a bit manipulative. But to each her own," Lee said, shrugging. "No coffee. Fresh out."

"You don't know me well enough to be so honest?" she replied hotly, journeying down a short hall to the living room, even though she'd seen most of it from the kitchen. Images of old diners and black and white pictures of chefs from maybe the twenties or thirties hung on the walls. Another bookshelf displayed large nature books and collectable cookbooks. "Did you get some of these from the pawn shop?"

"Some of what?"

"These old books."

"Thrift stores, mostly. Hey," he appeared behind her as she examined a decorative brown cover titled *The First American Cook-book*. "As I recall, Pauline, you don't like steak. I can make you grilled cheese—it's a magic bullet when hungover. I used to make them for the college students when I ran a place near campus."

"That sounds amazing," she said, realizing she no longer felt drunk. Following Lee back to the kitchen, she watched as he opened the fridge and pulled out gruyere and muenster cheeses, along with a huge block of white cheddar, then rummaged through an extensive collection of spices.

"It's funny that I'm spending time at The Grandview Inn and not eating a thing there. I never did like the food, to be honest. I just loved those sundaes. And the feel of the place. The ambiance. Like home."

"Like your childhood." He was busying himself shredding cheese into a bowl as he spoke.

"Maybe. My childhood was a mixed bag." She waited for him to respond, but he was focused. "Look at you!" she said, standing back to admire his dexterity in the kitchen. Pauline was never much of a cook. When Lissa was growing up, the poor girl would sneak most of the meals Pauline attempted on holidays to their golden retriever under the table and Michael would kindly lie as he complimented her lasagna or casserole—whatever she'd found on the internet that promised to be both comforting and low calorie. It was only low calorie because no one ate it.

"Let me tell you," Lee said, as he buttered the sprouted bread and placed slices of cheese at angles to ensure a nice, even distribution. "It takes commitment to get this kind of body." He rubbed his belly.

"You're in decent shape for a man your age," Pauline said, lifting an eyebrow. "I can see the remnants of muscles."

"I used to lift," he said, puffing out his chest a bit. "All through high school. I was a wrestler, runner, the whole thing."

"Did you bike?"

"I'll tell you a secret, Pauline," he said, leaning over the counter. "I never had a bike when I was a kid. They terrify me."

"That's sad."

Lee got a distant look on his face, then pressed the spatula over the bread, causing a delightful sizzle. "So, you're setting up your kid."

"I really found the perfect guy for her—the total opposite of her ex-husband."

"How do you know he's the perfect guy?" Lee asked, flipping the sandwich. The cast iron pan looked heavy.

"Guess it depends, but I'm pretty good at reading people,"

Pauline said. "I read that asshole Trent the moment I saw him, but Lissa was young and in love, and I didn't trust my instinct. I thought I was being overbearing. You know, most of the trauma people face comes from family members. And kids can cause trauma as often as parents, mostly because they magnify what you don't want to see about yourself."

"I was probably one of those kids who caused my parents trauma." He shook his head, "Whew! I was bad. Went to juvie a while and got worse. Nothing crazy."

"Let me guess." She assessed him. "Shoplifting?"

"I had a thing for cars. We were poor, so I'd break in to grab cash and other valuables—but after juvie I learned how to hotwire cars. That was the olden days and even then you could only do it with certain models."

"I don't think any form of prison in this country truly offers rehabilitation." As the buttered bread sizzled in the frying pan and cheese began to bubble, Pauline felt something overtake her. She thought about the hardening she'd seen in clients who had been released from prison, especially those who felt it unjustified. What might happen if Trent drove the few hours here? How could Lissa prepare—even if she did have a gun—if he caught her off guard? After what he'd done at The Lavender Center, after all those years in prison hardening him…

As Pauline tried to focus on Lee, she lost her balance. She suddenly realized the danger her daughter might be in. "I have to go," Pauline said abruptly, just as Lee was plating the best-looking grilled cheese she'd ever seen.

"Okay," he said, pausing. "I thought you still had a half hour or so. Want me to walk you back to your car?"

"Not sure I trust you around my car," she joked, side-eying him.

"Good one. If only we could go back in time, right?"

"Preach. No, no, don't worry about it. I'll take that beautiful sandwich to go though, if you can give me a paper towel or something."

"Take a bite in front of me?" he said.

Momentarily, she felt present again as she bit into the buttery bread toasted to a perfect light brown and savored the richness of melted cheese. Placing her free hand on her heart, she looked directly into Lee's warm eyes and said, "Will you marry me?" then immediately felt embarrassed by the joke.

"Maybe," Lee said, starting on another grilled cheese and patting his belly. A belly well-earned indeed, she thought. Then, gripping her keys, she rushed out as though propelled by a tough wind.

As she hustled back to the restaurant, she held her keys so tightly that they began to hurt her palm. When she saw her Subaru, she began to jog to her car and, grilled cheese still in hand, she started the ignition. For perhaps the first time in her life, Pauline ignored speed limit signs, weaving in and out of traffic. At a light, she thought to text her daughter and Cal.

"I was going to text you. I'm going to be late, so you're saying I shouldn't go?" Cal wrote in response to her previous text informing him she would be late. "It was a client call. Emergency."

"Raincheck," Pauline said, using the voice to text. She pushed on the gas a little harder and turned up "The Beautiful Ones." She hadn't so much as kissed Lee, but she already felt a certain intimacy with him. She took another bite of the sandwich. Everything was lined up at last, and after years of pain, collectively and personally, she was ready to experience a better world.

The gift-wrapped box rattled in the trunk as she navigated familiar roads to a house she'd only been to one time before, at Christmas, when her daughter was still engaged.

Trent

WordPress Entries

1.Sunday October 24

Well, here I am, starting a blog. Not sure what to name it yet. I guess it's about anger and business and how to come up in the world. I won't tell you my name, but I'll tell you I just got out of prison after too many days. I met a lot of fucked up people there & almost all of the most fucked up of them fucked with me. Years. Years of my life locked up for what? You guessed it. A woman.

I don't believe in a whole lot, but my family raised me to understand that no one in this world is going to fix anything for anyone. I have to do it myself and so do you.

I wrote to my mother every day like I was eight or something & told her about only the parts of prison that weren't too heinous to share. I didn't mention my ex, the reason I was there, but in her responses, she always did, which pissed me off. Eventually, I stopped writing. This is a good tip if you know someone in prison and write them. Don't just keep repeating the fact that they're in prison and don't keep replaying the story that landed them there. That is already going on in their heads, you know?

Anyway, there were also people who wrote me who I didn't know. Okay, one person. A woman, who said she was part of a writing program in college, getting her advanced degree. She told me that she got internship credit to write to prisoners, but she wasn't really sure what to say. I told her I could use a little encouragement, and if she could spare me any worldly news because our world seemed fucked, I'd appreciate it. She did. She sent me passages from essays by Seneca and Plato, philosophers who shared my values to an extent. I'd learned about them before but didn't think much of it. All these memes don't really sink in unless you really sit with them.

So fucking ironic. I worked hard to build my family's business, and now thanks to my own fucking temper and a bad choice in women, here I was leaving it up to my screwy little brother and aging father to keep it going. I was going to lose everything. I'll pick this up tomorrow. This is a quote by Seneca: "He who fears death will never do anything worthy of a man who is alive."

2. Monday October 25

I won't lie. There was a time when I first got locked up that all I wished was that I'd truly choked the life out of that bitch. The ex. She didn't understand how hard I'd worked for her, to support her. Every day was me putting in ten hours or more of labor, managing a bunch of unmanageable people in the middle of the summer with the midwestern heat. She was depressed like my mother used to be when I was younger & unsure of herself & there's nothing worse than that. Don't ever surround yourself with people like that. They bring you down.

There was no way she'd make it on her own, and I stayed because I was trying to help. So, why does she get to have the freedom? I hate weakness. Weakness should be the thing that we imprison people for. I never had the privilege to be weak. I never had anything given to me the way she had. And there she was for years working at a bike shop, then suspending kids like me for getting in fights.

The woman who wrote me seemed to have a sense of self. An identity. I was not stupid, just angry. Angry at so much of this world that seems so full of itself and so sorry for itself, and when that fucking pandemic hit it was like holding a magnifying glass to that anger and feeling of helplessness I saw all around me. I felt like an ant that might catch fire under it. I couldn't live in a repressed socialist regime. I lost it.

But by the time I knew I was getting out I was a new man. Rehabilitated, if you will. But not by these walls. Not by these asshole guards. Not by these other angry men who had stories that made them out as either heroes or victims. No. I was rehabilitated by the Stoics. By some woman who was getting her master's degree in writing of all things. She taught me how to write again. I know I'm not great, but I have some good ideas.

Hell, I even wrote her a poem toward the end that I won't share here, but it was pretty fucking good. She might be reading this blog. If so, thank you. You can reach out to me, you know. But I understand if you don't, what with all the school you have to do. Probably living in California or some shit anyway.

By the time I got out, I'd read more books than I had in school, and I felt more settled in who I was. I had no desire to go fuck with Lissa. I was over that shit. I realized that the only way to move forward is to forget the fucking past. Use it as a step to lift a motherfucker up.

"Waste no more time arguing what a good man should be. Be one." Marcus Aurelius said that, and that was my plan.

3.Wednesday October 27

I wasn't going to try to justify anything. That's what I told the judge because that's what he wanted to hear. I had a record now, but I still had my own fucking business, and my brother was going to ruin that if I didn't get out. I was ready for whatever when I was released. I didn't feel angry anymore. I felt like a man who needed to make up for lost time.

Nothing was stopping me. I am going to go local again, build up the business like I did before, only do it better. I have motivation. Like an athlete. I'm still young. I mean, I'm still kind of young, but this is what I was thinking, you know?

I'm going to find another woman. One that is more like my pen pal and less like that self-pitying bitch I married because she had a nice ass and tricked me into it. I had good intentions with her. I'm going to get the life I deserve.

When I got out and moved into my mother's house, it was like nothing changed at first. I was ready. Mom threw a barbeque and invited my old high school friends. We got a little drunk but not too much, and that night I lifted weights in the basement, same as I had in prison. I am in better shape than ever, and my mind is fierce. Focused. To be honest, a small part of me is a little grateful I'd gone to prison because now I feel so fucking strong. The world is mine.

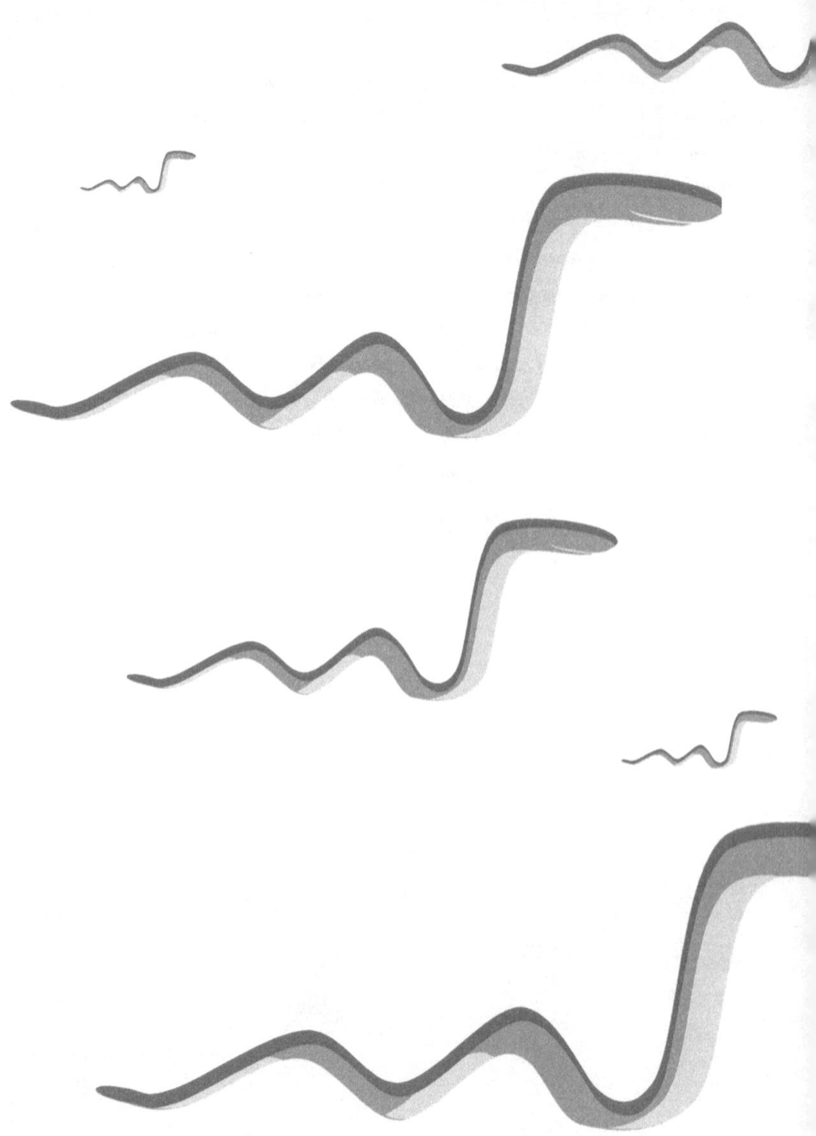

Release

Thursday October 28 (4:30 p.m.)

On his way home from work, Trent was driving his father's sturdy old Ford, the same car the family had owned since Trent was a child. He loved that old beater truck, the first one he'd driven when he began expanding the business, going from company to company passing out rack cards and flashing his perfect smile at the owners. He knew he was charming then, a night school student in his early twenties. Handsome. Confident. He looked more grizzled now, but he'd work with that.

After a twelve-hour day that began around 6 a.m., he was tired enough that Thursday that the road seemed to be waving at him. A cold beer awaited, his newly formed routine. He was thankful for the breeze that came in through the window. The F-150 hadn't had air conditioning since 2015. With two mowers in the back and an audio book by Zig Ziglar playing, Trent felt the adrenaline of a hard day's work. He was doing better. This is what it was about. The rest of it would come. A nice wife, one who was fertile, unlike Lissa, one who believed in herself and wouldn't fold under the weight of this ridiculous world. He'd have two kids, boys that looked just like him. He'd teach them how to run a business, and they'd do better than he had.

Since he'd got out of prison, Trent had been listening to old self-improvement and business books non-stop. In the last few days, he had read or listened to classics like *How to Think and Grow Rich, How to Win Friends and Influence People,* along with books about his heroes Steve Jobs, Elon Musk, and Jeff Bezos, who had changed the course of human history forever. The future was looking promising, and Trent was even thinking he might write his own book one day, after the company got big enough to brag about. He saw millions in the future. He could move his mother out of her two-bedroom house and into one of those nice developments for old people that had community activities and an onsite medical professional.

When he stopped to get gas, a black Subaru with tinted windows, just like his mother-in-law used to drive, pulled up too close behind him. He gave the driver the middle finger and filled up the tank, thinking if the guy got out for a fight he'd defuse it. Or just scare him and move on. He didn't have time for dumb shit like that anymore. But no one got out of the Subaru, and when Trent pulled away, it followed him.

Was some asshole really going to come at him over the middle finger? Really? But Trent had met people in prison who admitted to killing people over less, even just for the fun of it. He figured some of them were lying, but the stories were enough to make him pause. Dad's gun was always in the glove compartment. Since he was three blocks from his mother's house, he decided to pull over on the side of the road near an abandoned UDF and settle whatever this was. Maybe the Subaru would keep driving.

Trent readied himself for whatever was to come, feeling his heart pick up pace. He opened the glove compartment, but when he looked in the rearview and saw the older woman with bright pink glasses coming toward him, he began to laugh. It was his ex-mother-in-law, the drunk psychologist. She was probably around for some conference or something and wanted to see if it was him. She walked toward the glass and tapped on it.

"Long time," she said, as he rolled down his window. "I thought that might be you, but I wasn't sure."

"Pauline. Interesting to see you here. You headed downtown, or did you come out to see me?" Fleetingly, Trent wondered if he should've grabbed that gun after all. Maybe there was someone in the car with her. He checked the rearview and didn't see any sign of movement.

"No, I'm here for you," Pauline said. "I just wanted to come here to personally ask you to leave my daughter alone."

Trent opened the door and jumped down. "I have no business with Lissa. No desire at all to be anywhere near her," he said honestly. Even the sight of her mother made his stomach sour.

"You promise?" she said.

"What is wrong with you, lady?" he asked, running his palm over his face in frustration. "I have a restraining order. I have a business to run. Do you not see the mowers in back? I'm doing shit in the world, unlike your daughter. I have ambition. I have no desire to be near that sad ass bitch."

Pauline stared at him for a long time, nodding slowly, and something in Trent snapped then. He saw Lissa screaming, saying she'd kill him if he got near her. He saw something off in her mother's eyes and pushed her aside to get back in his truck.

Just as he was climbing back up, he felt a pinch at his lower back as the sound of a gun firing nearby rendered him momentarily deaf. The wave of numbness down the backs of his legs paralyzed him, and he felt the wetness of blood with his hand. Confused, he turned to look at Pauline, but she was gone. Instead, he saw a hallucination of his ex-wife, and he lunged toward her. "I was going to leave you alone," he growled. "I was going to move on."

Lissa

Friday, October 29

The store was about to close as she arrived. A new calf-height piece of agate sat just inside the door of TSH, a late arrival from the bulk purchases made back when the store was still turning a profit. Lissa paused to remove her jacket, rubbing her hands together briskly to remove the chill that lingered from the crisp day. She bent down to appreciate the stone's patterns, noticing that Annika had gone hard on the frankincense oils. The fragrance enveloped her, and a bit of the smoke caught in Lissa's throat. She walked toward her partner shakily, ready to sit down.

Pausing to attune herself to the space, Lissa felt a moment of reprieve. The only spirits in the shop were gentle. Sometimes, she'd feel Annika's parents nearby, watching out for her. Lately, with Lissa's anxiety on high alert and Trent's burdensome presence, moments of calm were rare. She wished this sense of peace would last, but Trent's voice arrived in her head again, telling her to stop being so sentimental and stupid.

Without saying hello, Lissa noticed Annika watching her, waiting. Some of the tension between the women melted when their eyes met. Lissa felt so feeble, and her friend likely picked up on that, or perhaps heard her brief thoughts of Annika's parents, but a serious conversation still needed to be had. Lissa pulled up one of the stools, reminding herself to be present. Annika had purchased these wooden stools ages ago at the thrift store and painted them silver. The legs were uneven, and Lissa felt the sensation of falling as she repositioned her weight.

"I need your help. I'm sorry, and I need your help," she started. Not the most graceful words, but they were honest.

Annika held her gaze. Empathy glimmered in her eyes, but before she had a chance to answer, the door flung open. Raven sighed loudly as he barreled in, looking slightly damp in sandals and an oversized tank top despite the weather. He removed a large hiking backpack and dropped it to the floor. The graying sky outside crept into the shop as Raven rummaged around, mumbling, finally retrieving a small box and dropping it next to Lissa.

"I was on mushrooms when I wrapped this piece, and it stole my aura. Do you still see one around me?" He turned to Annika. "Does the stone have it?"

"Your aura is fine," she said.

"Whew." He bent down and whispered in Lissa's ear, "Good to see you, my friend. This is the order for Tammy. Let me know how she likes it." After he excused himself to the bathroom, Lissa watched Annika shift her weight back to center.

"You were saying you were sorry?" Annika said. Her black eye-liner was smudged near the left eye. When Lissa had the thought, her friend traced the bottom of her lid with her middle pinky to smooth it out.

"You know what I'm trying to say, probably better than I do, but I don't feel—I don't know—myself, since the accident, and when I tell you why, you'll hate me forever, so, fuck it," Lissa told Annika.

Annika glared. "You think you killed him?"

"I'm desperate, and I need you. Your help," she pleaded.

Annika pulled up her stool and leaned forward to rest her chin on her fist. "You don't look like you just killed someone." She looked her straight in her eyes, her gaze piercing the space between them. "What did you do? You recited her mantra, didn't you? Do you understand now why I didn't want you getting ahead of yourself and messing with Inga?"

"You really want to patronize me right now?"

"Yes. I do," she said firmly. "Deal with it. You have to be strong enough to make the right decisions." Annika sat up straight, feeling a shot of adrenaline surge through her body as she balled her fists, just like her father used to.

"But that's just it. I didn't make the decision" she pleaded with her. "I just—there was an accident, and I saw him coming toward me in my mind, and I had to act. Because I knew the chant and I didn't have time to think twice, I just started. I repeated the chant, and pictured his heart slowing ..."

Annika began to pace, hands on her waist. "So, you're telling me you conducted magic from a place of fear. Craft 101: don't do that. Do you need me to make you a list?" Frustrated, she ran her hand through her hair. "Go on."

"I pulled up his Facebook page." She paused, fearing that saying the words out loud somehow made her more culpable. "He's dead." She held up her phone. "Shot, at least according to social media. And my body feels hollow. My anxiety is worse than ever—it's like he'll never leave me alone now, like he's taking over my every thought. Every time I try to sleep. Every quiet moment, I hear him—his footsteps, his keys, the way he always cleared his throat."

Annika examined the image of Trent and sucked her teeth.

"This is what he looked like up close, huh?"

"If he's really dead and you think you did it, that means he's got a right to a piece of you," Annika said. "And you offered it freely. You didn't kill him technically, so get that out of your head, but you put in the order, so to speak, and now he gets to fuck with you because you feel guilty. You have to find a way to release that guilt."

There was a loud crashing sound from the bathroom, then a call of assurance from Raven.

They turned back towards each other. "But he's dead," Lissa continued. "That's not reversable. He was a horrible person, and I felt like it was self-defense in a way."

"Now you're justifying it?" Annika asked, incredulous.

"I'm not. I feel horrible, but he can't haunt me forever, right?" Lissa realized Annika was looking at her in a way she never had before, almost as though she were a specimen in a lab.

"Trent's a spirit, and spirits don't play by rules. He's probably not even sure what he's capable of yet, since he's new to the realm. Do you remember what happened at TLC after he ran that night?" Annika asked.

Lissa nodded, recalling the calm way Doreen and Glenda had cast a spell without a hint of malice or ill intent toward him, only a lens of protection and justice.

"That was the kind of magic that doesn't backfire. Glenda cornered him. She called on nature, and he got lost in the woods near the mother tree. She tripped him with her roots and held him in place. It was just enough time for the police to arrive, but he wasn't hurt and wasn't sentenced to anything beyond what he'd truly done. That made sense. Putting up a shield makes sense. Strengthening yourself makes sense. Stopping him from coming near you makes sense. But killing him or manipulating his thoughts or actions is not our kind of magic. You fucked with the natural order of things by going to Inga, and you fucked yourself by casting that spell."

"I didn't think I could really do it, Annika" Lissa pleaded with her. "I didn't think it would work. I'm not powerful like you."

"I can't communicate with spirits. You're a gifted medium, Lissa." She softened. "You can tap other realms, and that is deep magic. Every single thing you do with intention has the potential to be deep magic. You know the principles. Now, your gift is your weakness. Because you can tap other realms, he's able to haunt you."

"You really think I'm gifted?"

Annika bit her top lip and let the silence say its piece first.

"Why do you think we call this place TSH, The Spirit House? If we named it after me, it'd be called The Surly Psychic."

Lissa hadn't heard messages from her grandmother or father in years. When she was a child, it was an everyday thing to hear stories or singing as she tried to dodge balls in gym class or to hear her grandmother's voice when she'd spend time in the mirror examining her crooked teeth. *"Peck yer 'ead oep, girl. Yer beautifoel."* Her earliest memory was of the day one of Pauline's friends arrived with a bundt cake and condolences after her father died. She'd been speaking to him every day since he died, but he'd never spoken back until Pat asked her if she wanted a piece of cake. "No thank you, Pat," Lissa had said that day, as politely as her father taught her.

"No thank you, Aunt Pat," she'd responded, removing her sunglasses.

That was when her father arrived, and her great-grandmother's voice stopped. He was all decked out in his favorite biking outfit, as visible as if he were in the 3D, right in front of her. He told her she didn't have to call this woman anything. He told her to stand her ground then and always, so she straightened her shoulders and placed her hands on her waist like she'd seen Pauline do. "I'd like to call you Pat from now on."

Pauline laughed at the assertion and the two women exchanged a shrug. "Well, alright then," Pat said. "If you ever change your mind." Lissa's father had only shown up a few more times in her life, and each time he was less visible, then also becoming inaudible. She still felt his presence till she graduated, and when she looked out on the crowd the day she received her high school diploma, sure he'd show up for this final event to send her off, she knew what she'd previously felt and seen was gone. He'd moved on, and instead of being sad, she understood.

Since that day, spirits became a more subdued background music in her life, entities to scan for and check on, just to make sure they weren't getting into trouble, like Tammy's kid. She could talk to them, but there was no reasoning, and often they were on their way out, anyway. There was a short window for most, and the heartbreaking ones, the small children, hung on the longest. She hadn't heard or seen anything but Trent today. "What can I do now? Should I go back to Inga?" Lissa asked.

"No!" Annika threw her hands up.

"How is she not tortured herself for doing this kind of magic, if it's torturing me?" Lissa asked quietly.

"That woman feels no guilt." Annika's voice hardened. "Look, I have to say it one last time, then I'll stop. I told you! Damn it." Annika stomped her foot like a child, then began to pace the store again, cursing under her breath. A customer started to open the door, and when she saw the look on Annika's face, she closed it again, backing away, eyes wide.

"I told you about manipulation when you wanted to force someone to buy that damn lingam stone." Annika turned back towards her and paced faster. "I should have seen it coming. I tried to help you."

"Tried to help? You acted like it was no big deal that he was getting out." Lissa regretted saying it as soon as the words came out of her mouth.

"You have no idea," Annika replied through gritted teeth.

Confused, Lissa shrugged. "What do you mean?"

"Later."

"Great. So, now I'm cursed forever." She said it as a plea for help, not a statement, but she heard the sound of a key scraping across the counter again, as though pressing against her bones. "He was already haunting me when he was alive. I was already afraid, already tortured, but now he has what he wanted. I feel fragmented."

Annika stopped moving and took a huge breath in through her nose, then sighed. She turned to Lissa and cupped her face in one hand, squeezing, staring into her eyes in a way no one ever had. The two women stood like this for seconds or minutes, Lissa couldn't tell. Finally, Annika's energy softened, as did her voice. They both willfully ignored Raven's slow clap from the hallway. "I forgive you," Annika said finally. "We'll have to consult the books and do some digging. I doubt we have anything here, but we need to move."

"I know a shaman," Raven said with his hand up from the back of the room, inserting himself in the conversation even though he had no idea what was going on.

"No thanks," Annika told him without even looking back. She began searching for something in the books behind the counter as Lissa tried to suppress Trent's screaming within her. His words were indistinguishable, and she covered her ears, folding her body over as though she could duck beneath the sound. "There's nothing here. Okay, so you said you feel like two people. Two lives or two versions of one life? Everything else or just you?" She pulled a Moleskine from a hidden pocket in her jacket and reached for a pen.

Lissa looked down at the small bells that hung from the bottom of her wispy skirt. She tried to focus. Her toes were painted a bright yellow that her mother had chosen because it was a happy color.   "Two versions of one life, I guess. One is haunted."

Pauline had insisted they both paint their nails to perk up the mood. She always dressed in loud prints, and, like her glasses, her nails matched almost every outfit she wore. She believed in the therapeutic nature of color and statement pieces, unlike her daughter, who stuck to grays and blacks. As Lissa stared down, the nails didn't seem to belong to her.

"What exactly did you chant?" Annika stopped writing and widened her stance. She rolled up her sleeve, exposing the tattoo of an owl on her forearm, her familiar.

Lissa remembered Annika's look of calm resolve when she had walked into the room the night Trent tried to break into The Lavender Center. Lissa had been losing oxygen, feeling a swell at her temples as though something in her would soon pop, as the grip tightened around her neck intensified. Trent had the upper hand. He was everywhere and being outnumbered no longer mattered. She remembered the feeling of his rough hands releasing her throat when Annika and Glenda burst into the room that day. She remembered closing her eyes as her breath and energy thinned, melting underneath his grip, as she recited a mantra no one taught her. One she'd thought had come true. I wish I could start over.

Lissa cleared her throat and began to stand, telling herself more than anyone. "It was protection, self-defense. I didn't even know the full ritual when I recited it, it just came to me with the vision of him coming toward me. The same way it did that day when you found me by the window. I remember wishing I could begin again. Wishing I could start over and that he was not in my world, then I recited what I remembered." She wrote down the chant.

Annika read the spell, then stared deeply into her friend's eyes again, as though searching for the full story, the same way she had when they first met. Only this time she looked deeper, as though trying to uncover something specific, a subtle bend of light. "I see him. He's replaying it. He's choking you in the memory space, trying to keep you where you separated from yourself many times. You are leaving your body as a method of self-preservation. You need to stay and fight."

They both heard a scraping at the front door, like someone was dragging a key across the wood. It went on for a while before the door flung open and a familiar-looking woman in a dark green suit and flower print shirt offered a waxy smile. Her heels were tall, shiny, and appeared to require both foot contortion and incredible balance. The woman strode toward Lissa and plopped a few hundred down on the counter. Her coiffed hair and perfect face were still, as though she were a walking statue. "Fuck it. I'll take that one." She pointed a manicured figure towards the corner.

"The lingam stone?" Lissa asked, surprised at both her sudden arrival and at the prospect of such a big sale. She could hear Trent laughing, as if he were in her head.

The woman nodded, looking bored.

"Yes, ma'am," Lissa said, springing to action but wishing she could feel happier in this moment. A month's rent in a single transaction. "We're so glad you came in. I've seen you around the neighborhood."

"I work for the law firm across the street."

It was the woman whose eyes Lissa had met the day Ash had arrived at the store. Annika headed toward the back for a dolly. Raven said, "You might need help getting this into your place. We can take it out to your car for you. This stone offers the powers of the universe, boundless creative energy, and strength."

"I'm sure it does," the redhead said flatly.

Lissa tried to smile. "Why did you decide to come back for the stone?"

"It's like something came over me last week. I was walking past, and I felt a tug toward the shop. I didn't have time to stop just then, but I decided then and there it had to be mine."

Annika stared at Lissa, likely hearing her ask herself *Did I cast a spell on this woman, too?* Pushing the thought out of her mind, she asked, "Raven, can you please help ..." She looked at the receipt. "Mrs. Smith out to her car?"

"I can help you the whole way, if you'd like," he said, offering his easy smile to the new customer, which the woman seemed to receive well.

Coyly, she replied, "I'd appreciate that."

Once the two were gone, Annika got a look of pure focus and tucked a few books in her bag. "I'll get in touch with our reinforcements."

"Glenda and Doreen?"

"Minimum. I think we should close post haste. Until we fix this, don't leave your place. Keep your sheilds up."

As Lissa turned off the lights, she turned to her friend, grateful to have her back.

Pauline

Saturday, October 30

It took two days for Pauline to reschedule her meeting with Cal. As she weaved in and out of traffic, heading to Lissa's apartment, she couldn't shake the idea that her daughter hated her for not making the date or had some sort of inclination about what Pauline had been doing, trying to set them up. Then again, Lissa was never one who just showed up at the front door, and she hadn't reached out to say anything, like stop, or why, so it was doubtful. Impossible that she knew.

Knowing the fragility of her daughter's traumatized brain, Pauline pressed the gas harder, wanting to beat Cal to her daughter's apartment. Like usual, Pauline would have to intervene. She dialed Cal's number on the way.

"I'm sorry again for rescheduling so last minute," she told him. "Thank you." Pauline gave him directions to Lissa's apartment, which was only a few miles away from where he lived, he told her.

"Pauline, that cancelation was okay—I was running late. You sure your daughter likes sushi?"

"Yes! It's her favorite. Get some vegan rolls, too. She doesn't always listen to me, so I'll stop with the endless gratitude, but once again … thank you. Um." Pauline paused. "I'm going to get there first, so if you need help with the food, just text."

"Will do."

She ended the call just as she was pulling up to Lissa's house. "Honey? Honey, I'm here," Pauline called when she arrived at Lissa's front door. She knocked and knocked again, then used her spare key. The apartment was a mess. There was a to-go container on the counter from the Grandview Inn that smelled rancid. She searched the receipt for the date/time and, sure enough, it was from two days ago. "Lissa!" Throwing the container away, Pauline covered her nose with her arm as she searched frantically for something to spray in the room to remove the smell of old fish.

When her daughter staggered out of the bedroom with disheveled hair and sleepy eyes, Pauline furrowed her brows. She smelled smoke and could see a row of candles lit in the bedroom. "Where were you?" Lissa asked.

"Where were you? I told you we'd be over today. I left like three messages."

"We?"

"Cal is on his way," she cried, exasperated. "You agreed to all this. Dr. Gregory. You said you were up to rescheduling today."

"But I just saw him." She staggered a bit, her eyes still sleepy.

"Well, I guess we should clean up."

"Huh? What is wrong with you, honey?" She took a moment to take in more of her surroundings, at the mess and chaos of the room.

"I'm fine," Lissa said, unconvincingly, as Pauline stared at a pentagram carved into a burning pillar candle on the mantel, wax dripping to the floor. There was a small knife next to it.

"Yeah, you're far from fine," Pauline said, sighing. She jumped when she saw something move in the corner of the room. A cat sauntered toward her. "Um. You got a cat, honey?" She bent down to scratch his ears and saw that he had a collar. "Do you want me to text Cal and tell him to turn around? He's getting us sushi."

"Maybe, but I need food." Lissa began picking up clothes that were draped over the couch and sprayed the apartment with a citrus concoction she made as Pauline began to rinse the dishes that sat in piles next to the sink.

The window near the kitchen had a clear view of the street, and Pauline watched for Cal's car. "Honey, I know you're upset," she called out as she scrubbed. "I think everything will be okay now though. I do." She loaded the dishwasher and wiped her hands on a towel, then scanned the apartment. They'd tidied everything up rather quickly, and Lissa was sitting, petting her cat. "Here, drink some water." Pauline thrust a glass of water in her hands.

Lissa nodded, smoothing out her wrinkled clothes with her hands.

Cal's Tesla glided up to the curb a few minutes later, and Pauline watched as he found a parking space and went to the trunk to retrieve the food. Usually, people had trouble finding the place, but Cal seemed to move through the world with ease.

"He's here, honey. I'll be right back." Pauline darted to the door without pause and waved him forward, signaling to Cal that he could come in when he was ready before ducking back into the dark apartment. She rushed toward her daughter, fighting the urge to fix her hair.

"Hello. May I come in?" he asked, standing awkwardly at the door.

"Um. Good to meet you," Lissa said, looking to Pauline as though asking her to lead the conversation.

"A man who shows up with food is a good man," Pauline said, clapping her hands together and moving to take the bags of food from Cal's hands. She hurried into the kitchen with the food, calling over her shoulder, "I'll let you two re-introduce yourselves to each other."

"Cal," Lissa said, looking at her retreating mother. "I think my mother is trying to set us up, and it's awkward. I just wanted to get that out of the way." She looked up at him. "Also, I've been a bit … ill, so pardon my apartment."

"Nah," he waved his hand. "Looks great to me. I like the painting." Cal pointed to a painting Pauline had purchased for Lissa at an arts festival they attended shortly after she left TLC. It was the image of an elderly woman's hands upturned, the lines of her palms in different colors. Pauline thought the painting was odd, but she remembered Lissa telling her how many stories she could see in such a simple image.

"It's a favorite," Lissa said with the hint of a smile.

"I brought vegan sushi at your mother's request, and I asked them to put in whatever they wanted for the rest of it. We got a boat, I guess," he said. "I don't eat sushi too often."

"I'll set the table," Pauline said, eager to busy herself again and leave the two on their own. She paused in front of Lissa to give the girl's forearm a squeeze. If only she could tell her daughter just how safe she was now.

"Thank you both," Lissa said. "I have chopsticks if you want. They're by the fridge." She called out to Pauline in the kitchen.
Cal immediately followed and began to help Pauline, and she caught him sneaking glances at her daughter, who wasn't paying attention. As silly as it was, she kept willing Lissa to look up before catching herself—now here she was embracing magical thinking.

Lissa took a seat, releasing her hair from a messy ponytail, and nodded. "I am hungry. I feel like I haven't eaten in days."

Have you? Pauline wanted to ask.

"I'm starving myself," Cal said, patting his belly. "So, your mother tells me you're a small business owner."

"I co-own a shop, so yes. A business owner like most of the world since the pandemic incentives," Lissa said. "But we're struggling lately. People seem to be relying on all these health apps."

Cal swallowed hard. "RoboHealth?"

Lissa nodded. Pauline took a few steps back and assessed. Did the girl already know? She definitely wasn't acting like herself, but how could she know?

Cal sheepishly admitted to being a part of the development of that app. "I was part of the team that launched it. I even recruited a few of my friends for a test study. It all seemed so innocent then, like any other meditation app. It wasn't till recently that they began to discuss how dangerous it was for patients to blindly trust algorithms that were not equipped to fully process the human brain. Everything in that app is positive, but only if a patient has the right tools, right doctor?" He turned to look at Pauline.

Pauline nodded absently. "A lot of discussion, yes." It had been a common gripe from the community, but as the two stared at Pauline as though waiting for elucidation or some interesting perspective, she remained uncharacteristically silent.

Lissa plucked a thin piece of cucumber from a roll, then set down her chopsticks. She hadn't eaten a thing.

"Well, I think I'll hit the road and maybe we can reschedule for a better time?" Cal had asked.

"No! Stay for dessert." Pauline replied too quickly as she watched her daughter take unenthusiastic bites of an avocado roll and could see that Lissa was empty, somehow. A void. She looked like she had when she was released from the hospital.

"I'm honestly stuffed. Rice sneaks up on me," he said. As Cal turned to leave, Pauline asked as she followed him to the door. "Don't you want to take any leftovers?"

"No thanks." He traced a circle over his belly.

"Okay, raincheck." Pauline stood as Cal walked to the door.

"I'd love to." He leaned to look past Pauline at Lissa and said, "I'd love to see you again, too, Lissa, if you feel the same way" he said, holding her gaze for a moment.

Noticing a pentagram drawn in charcoal on a piece of paper on the table, Pauline angled her body to shield him from it and leaned into Cal just as he was about to leave. "Sorry about the girl. She's going through a lot."

He whispered back. "She's perfect."

Lissa smiled from her seat at the table, and as soon as the doctor was gone turned to her mother with wide eyes. Suddenly, her voice was crystal clear, as if she had somehow returned to her body. "Where were you when it happened?" Lissa demanded. "Where was I?"

"Wasn't he amazing, Lissa? Like I said?" She clapped her hands together, smiling. "And what is that?" She motioned to the pentagram, her smile quickly turning to a frown.

"Where have you been, Mom? I think I might've been the reason …"

"I had to go out of town for a client emergency. I'll tell you about it later, but first, tell me about you. You look like a piece of cardboard, honey. It's like you're trying to hide out. Tell me what's going on." Pauline braced herself a long moment as her daughter appeared to search for the right words. When they finally came, they spilled out.

"He's dead, Mom. Trent—"

"Oh. Oh, honey," Pauline said embracing her daughter.

"I did it," Lissa sobbed. "I killed him."

"Wait, what?" Pauline squeezed her daughter tighter before letting her go and leading her to the couch. Pauline looked back at the rancid carryout, then moved the paper with the charcoal pentagram to the side table.

"He'll never leave me alone, Mom. Not now. I killed him, and I can't live with that. He won't let me. He'll haunt me, torture me, and rightfully so. I'm not sure who pulled the trigger, but I made it happen. It was my order."

"Honey, you're not making sense. You might be in shock." Pauline examined her daughter's eyes and was jolted back to what she'd seen in them those years ago when Trent left her daughter bloodied and bruised. She felt her body tighten. "Honey, he deserved to go to prison, and the world was probably better for it. But you didn't do it. You tried to save him."

Lissa pulled away, examining her mother. "According to the post, he was shot."

"I know, honey."

"How? How do you know?"

Annika

Saturday, October 30

Lissa was never late. She was annoyingly punctual, in fact, and even more annoyingly, she never pointed out Annika's perpetual tardiness. She was too polite to do so. At least, she had been. Annika was mulling over the idea that perhaps she'd been a bit too hard on her friend. Sure, Lissa had fucked with the natural course of the universal flow, but what human hadn't? What witch hadn't? And, more, what human hadn't acted out of desperation when they were afraid?

She unpacked a small box of decorative candles from a local vendor. As she added tiny round price stickers to their bottoms and positioned them on display, she called TLC and was put on hold when she asked to speak to an owner. The recorded message was Glenda's reassuring voice, explaining that TLC was a place of whole-body healing, and that there was no cookie-cutter answer for people who had been through trauma. "We work with every person at a soul level," she was saying when the line finally transferred.

"This is Doreen," a sing-song voice said. Annika paused, waiting. "Ah, my dearest, how are you?" she added knowingly.

"I'm not great," Annika sighed. "Do you have time to talk?"

"I always time for you, Annika. We have Ceremony tomorrow. You're coming, right?"

"I was going to, but I was hoping to get your advice about Lissa. I don't think I can bring her tomorrow. She practiced bad magic, even after all my warnings." After explaining the full situation to Doreen, lacing the story with expletives and apologies, Annika caught her breath and waited.

"You're personalizing," Doreen said seriously, which caught Annika off guard.

"Wait, what?"

"You are offended that she didn't listen to you. But you need to remember that this isn't about you. This is a time for patience," Doreen said. Patience. Trust.

"But can we trust her after this?"

"She needs us, and her own magic more than ever. Bring her tomorrow, dear. We can help. But you can only help her if you forgive. You have to work out your anger. Punch a pillow or something." She explained that the only thing she could do to help her friend was to drive her out to the TLC for the four of them to cast a circle together again, as they had in residence so many years ago. There was high magic, Doreen told her, but it couldn't be done alone or in a pair. It needed sacred space that had been nurtured.

"I understand. Is tomorrow safe, though?"

"Samhain is the perfect opportunity to deal with spirits, but it is also their most potent time. It might not be easy to get her out here, but you can do it. We will help from here," she assured Annika. "Together, we can draw strength from each other and the land. Meet us by the mother tree."

Every morning during their time at TLC, Annika had watched Glenda journey outside in her robe, barefoot, to give an offering to the trees and land near the firepit. She and Doreen would meditate for hours, chanting and infusing the area with light before and after ceremonies. It was a dedication Annika hadn't seen by witches she knew in the city, who dabbled, posting to Instagram when they bought a new athame. By contrast, Glenda and Doreen showed a devotion like those she'd read about in the monastic tradition when she studied religion in college. *A true teacher makes you want to seek your own answers.*

Raven, who'd stopped by again, was less dependable on the register, sometimes messing up change or wandering away without notice, but Annika didn't have a choice. She left him in charge and told him to only take payment via apps. "I have to go check on Lissa."

Raven ran his fingers through his shoulder-length hair and nodded. "Sure, yes, Lissa's been keyed up, right? I'll hold down the fort. I have some wrapping to do." His tanned legs swung like a child's might from the wood stool he balanced on. His eyes were barely open, and Annika wondered if he might fall.

"No drugs, Raven."

"I don't do drugs. I only place my ear to mother earth and ingest her gifts as she instructs."

"No mushrooms, Raven."

He smiled a little, then gave her a look that suggested she was ridiculous, but that he'd acquiesce. Just as she was leaving, she heard the store's phone ring. "You're the boss. Hey, do you remember that show? It was about a boss, and it had Tony Danza in it. Wasn't it called You're the Boss or something?" The phone continued to ring, but Annika could hear his thought loop. He was running down the characters, wondering if Alyssa Milano was going to be in another sitcom one day. Were there still sitcoms, he wondered.

"Raven!" she called out to him, snapping her fingers. "Phone. No Alyssa Milano."

"Gotcha!" He looked around for the phone and put it on the speaker. "The Spirit House. This is Raven. How can I support you on your earthly journey? … Ah, yes, we have ceremonial candles. Anything you need. Open till …"

"Till 9 p.m., unless you have to close earlier than that to be somewhere," Annika whispered. "Don't forget to set the security code—and if you need me, text," Annika said.

"I'll be here till Midnight," he told the person on the phone.

Annika hesitated but left anyway. Maybe he'd sell some things. Brushing a thumbprint off the plaque on the door, she navigated the narrow hallways that led to the parking lot and drove fast, until she skidded her Jeep to a stop in front of Lissa's condo.

Rushing up to the door, Annika knocked for a few minutes. Something felt off. She couldn't get a read on Lissa's thoughts from outside. Instead, she got a flash of a man, grinning. A man she'd never even seen in person but knew instantly was Trent.

"Hello," a man said from behind her. He was walking a tiny black dog along the side of the road.

Startled, she turned, "Hello. Have you seen my friend who lives here? Lissa?"

"Not in days. She walks a lot. Always so sweet, Lissa. She bakes me a purple cake on my birthdays. Lavender and lemon. Sounds like soap, but it's damn good. I look forward to it all year." When his dog lunged toward a squirrel, he stumbled forward, his arm pulled forward. "This is my wife's dog, and she never walks it because of this. Tell her Paul says hay-lo."

After Paul turned the corner, Annika glanced around. Everything was too quiet. She moved around the bushes and tried to see in the side window, but the blinds were down, and it was dark inside. She scrambled for her phone and called her—she could hear Lissa's ringtone through the window. The condo was attached only on one side, so she walked around to where there was another door that led from the kitchen to the garbage cans. She knocked there first, then tried the door, which was also locked. "Lissa," she called into the bay window toward the back of the building, seeing a flickering light. A candle. Pushing her fingers beneath the small ledge of the window, she lifted up with all that she had in her and was surprised when the window opened swiftly, almost slamming at the top to expose only a screen. She punched at the corner of the screen, and it gave way. She climbed in, scraping her legs. Hearing Ash's soft mewing as he padded toward her, she struggled to stand. He tilted his head, confused, before turning swiftly as though to invite her to follow.

After closing the outside window and locking it, Annika rushed to follow the cat, who was now mewing and circling Lissa's limp body, which was lying on the floor in the living room. She let out a small gasp, rushing over to her friend. Not sneezing or struggling to breathe as she did around ordinary cats, Annika bent down and looked him in the eye. "Thank you," she started to say, but before the words were released from her lips, Ash rushed over to the kitchen and paced in front of the freezer, so Annika followed him and grabbed an ice cube, returning to her friend and tracing the ice gently over her forehead. Lissa's skin was hot to the touch. She could feel the heat emanating from her when her body began to make small movements, almost too subtle to see.

"He's here, inside my head. He's screaming at me nonstop. I can't stay here," she mumbled, her voice barely audible.

"You have to. You have to stay here." Annika urged, holding her hand tightly.

Lissa's eyes rolled back as Annika shook her. "We're going to visit Glenda and Doreen. We're going to get you help." She felt desperate.

"I can't," Lissa whispered. "I'm stuck. What if he won? He broke me, and I became just like him."

"No." Annika replied firmly.

Ash mewed and batted at Lissa's hand. Annika said, "You too, Ash. We might need you. Lissa, get up. Get. Up." Annika began to circle Lissa's body, chanting "Rise, rise, up and toward the sun, we are one with destiny. We must rise as one." She lifted her arms up, hands toward the sky, and summoned in the goddess. She could feel the support of Lissa's grandmother, the repetition of a saying, *Der is no pain, 'owever great, dat does naut ebb.* The woman's voice was like an instrument in itself. The phrase kept repeating, until a jolt of energy surged through Annika's heart. Ash pounced on Lissa's chest when she took a sharp breath, her whole body seizing off the floor, before falling back into a liminal space.

Cal

Saturday, October 30

Lissa searched for her hand, for any physicality, but she seemed to be without body. She saw her mother's co-worker. Cal placed his head in his hands and took a few deep breaths, trying to clear his head after his last client. The woman seemed to have worn him down. Lissa felt her energy getting closer, until she felt herself merge with Cal. Unsure if she was imposing a story or actually hearing his thoughts, she tuned into his inner monologue.

He was sad, thinking about his last client who'd lost both her daughters in the last three years, one to a car accident and the other to cancer, and her pain was palpable. It still seemed Cal had absorbed some of it in their session. While it wasn't the most measurable phenomenon, Cal knew that energy lingered, so he cracked the window to let in some of the crisp fall to air.

"I said I wouldn't do this anymore. I have to set firmer boundaries," he told himself, looking around and imagining what he might be doing if he hadn't come in today. While nothing exciting came to mind, even a trip to the hardware store to finally get that leaf blower this year would've been nice. Usually, after clients, Cal took a few minutes to reorient. He'd read about a meditation technique in which you simply listen—an underutilized skill by most people, even, sadly, psychologists. While using this technique, as you listen, you begin to expand your ability to hear, becoming aware of subtlety. To expand your ability to hear the more subtle rumblings beyond your immediate surroundings, you find more presence in the space you occupy. Now, he listened for birdsong, for a car alarm that was sounding blocks away, for the bounce of rubber on pavement, then blacktop.

Cal wondered about Lissa, as he'd been in the habit of doing lately. He couldn't stop thinking about her and what kind of stories she must hear from her clients. Perhaps some of the same people. Surely, people came to her with emergencies as well, likely with similar aims as those who seek counseling. He imagined that energy work, described rather cryptically on her website, was the process of trying to help a client shift emotional states. In his reading on mindfulness and his somewhat regular meditation practice, he'd begun to think differently about the ways people can get a handle on emotions, but it still felt somewhat unreachable for some. He used to think progress necessarily took years of psychotherapy, but now he believed in the potency of focus and attention. So long as the person was willing.

Maybe he was giving Lissa too much credit, but even in the short time he'd interacted with her, he'd noticed there was something special about her. She had seemed distracted, yes, in pain, but there was something else about her. Almost like she was heading somewhere he wanted to go. He stared out at a basketball court that sat across the street at a local community center and watched as a pair of middle schoolers missed basket after basket. When one finally made it, he cheered, not realizing someone had entered his office.

"Sir?" a woman's voice said from behind him. "Are you Dr. Gregory?"

Shit. So much for paying attention to the sounds around me, he thought. "I am." Cal turned around, realizing how distracted he was. When he saw the two police officers standing in wide-legged power poses, which struck Cal as a bit humorous, though surprised, he followed up with a smile and hello. They stared at him seriously, until his smile melted. "How can I help?"

"I'm Officer Brady, this is Officer Dillon," the shorter of the two replied.

"Good to meet you."

"We're not here for niceties," said Officer Dillon, a clean-shaven man who looked like a sophomore in high school. "Do you know Pauline Williams—Dr. Williams?"

"I do. She was a colleague. She's retired now, though, so she isn't around."

"We know. Do you happen to know where Dr. Williams was Thursday evening?" Officer Brady asked, all emotion masked from her face.

"No, actually." Cal felt his face scrunch. He gestured for the officers to sit, but they chose to remain standing, their power posing no longer humorous in the least. "We, um, were supposed to meet at the Grandview Inn, but she canceled at the last minute. She had a client call."

"You just said she was retired," Officer Dillon said.

"Well, yes, but sometimes the clients still reach out to her."

"Did she route a call to you?" Officer Brady asked as Officer Dillon began wandering around the office, pausing to open a window.

"No. And I couldn't tell you any details if she had," Cal said, glancing back.

"What time were you supposed to meet for dinner?"

"5 p.m."

"And what time did she cancel?"

"About quarter after 5 p.m., actually. I was on a call with a client, so I had just arrived when I got her text. Dr. Williams and her daughter were both supposed to be there. I hadn't met the daughter—erm, Lissa—before, but I was pretty sure I saw her leaving the restaurant when I pulled up, at about 6 p.m."

"Did you hear from Dr. Williams after that text?" Officer Brady was going down her list of questions, methodically.

"Yes. She asked me over to her daughter's apartment two days later. I brought sushi, but I didn't stay long."

"Why not?"

"Her daughter seemed caught off guard. I don't think Dr. Williams had given her much notice that I was coming. It was something of a setup, to be honest."

"What do you mean by set up?"

"Like a blind date." Cal shrugged.

"Did you notice anything odd about Dr. Williams's behavior that day?" Officer Dillon asked from across the room.

"No." Cal turned to look at him. "She was worried about her daughter."

"Interesting. Is there anything else you can tell us about Dr. Williams? Any other correspondence between Thursday night and now?"

"Am I allowed to ask what's going on here?"

Officer Dillon came up a little too close behind Cal. "We are investigating the murder of Trent Holden, which took place on Thursday evening. He was shot in the back while getting into his truck, a few miles from his residence. The bullet hit his kidney. Mr. Holden was recently released from prison. There is reason to believe Dr. Williams might be able to answer some questions for us. Do you know her?"

"Not really. Please let me know if I can help. I wish I knew more," Cal said, thinking about the image of Lissa from Pauline's desk, remembering the look in her eye, as though searching for a way out. It was as though she hadn't slept when they met in person, and he wondered if she was just a tortured soul. He'd met a few in his day, folks who seemed to invite the chaos of the universe in, and he wondered if she was capable of murder. The officers asked a few more questions that Cal answered robotically as he tried to understand what was happening. There was no way Pauline was capable of murdering someone, and he couldn't imagine Lissa doing so either, not that he knew her all that well. She had looked pretty off-kilter, but more tired than anything.

As the officers left, he re-played everything he could remember of that evening in his mind: the way Lissa had seemed to just be waking up, the odd smell in her apartment. If he'd been there to diagnose the situation, he would've guessed she was just going through a tough time. Nothing major had happened. She didn't seem particularly paranoid or anxious. Meanwhile, Pauline hadn't seemed distracted at all. She had seemed excited, hyper-focused and a little worried, but watchful, like a mother might be when hoping to set her daughter up on a date.

He remembered the way Lissa had looked deeply into his eyes and how radiant she had seemed despite everything, as though there were another person deep inside her. He wondered if he was allowed to call Pauline. Probably. Walking back to the window, he glanced out at two young men playing basketball and bit down on his bottom lip, not realizing he was doing it hard enough to cause a little droplet of blood to surface.

Unknown
Astral

Slowly coming back to consciousness, Lissa heard her friend say, "It's time to gather."

Glenda and Doreen had sent instructions, which Annika relayed as she gently stroked her friend's face. *Prepare with a ritual bath and a remembrance. Meditate. Focus.* The instructions continued as Lissa's eyes fluttered open and then closed again.

"I'm not ready to come back," Lissa said. "I need to sleep." She noted Annika's worried glance as she fell back into the safety of the blackness, then somewhere else entirely. The past.

Lissa grew up with magic, but it was always buried, a secret to be kept from her mother. She remembered the day her father saw the future, though she didn't realize it at the time. What she did know, always, was that he understood. He saw and heard what she did. She wondered if he'd known the day of his prediction. He must've known. And it must've terrified him.

The oil from an old Trek bicycle chain covered Lissa's tiny hands and forearms. At six, she strutted like a tiny mechanic in her brown overalls, with matted hair and a self-satisfied grin that faded when she went to rub her eyes. Just after she made contact—a moment too late—her father, Michael, swooped her slight body up into his arms, rushing her to the sink just as she began to scream.

"Shhhh. Let's get you cleaned up," he said in the same melodic voice he used to tell her stories at night. He grabbed a wad of paper towels from the counter and dampened them to wipe away the WD-40 that was smeared across her face. She could feel the thickness of the oil and tried to touch her face again, but her father grabbed her hand. "Stay still."

He crouched down to retrieve a few baby wipes from under the sink and gently cleared what the water wouldn't remove. Her eyelids fluttered and stung, but eventually she could open them again, allowing in blurred lights, then shapes. Her tears stopped stinging and began to feel normal again as her face dried and the thick smell dissipated.

"So. Tell me. What were you working on behind my back?" her father said.

"Bike chain," Lissa explained, blinking away tears.

"Bike chain, eh?"

She nodded. "I fixed it." She narrowed her eyes and scanned the kitchen, leaning slightly forward to glance into the living room, wondering if her mother might have returned.

"Your mother is still out with a client, don't worry." Lissa knew she was lucky Pauline had been called away before this incident, and she felt a stiffness in her body release. Her faint brows softened as she looked at her father and lifted her chin. He wiped a few more specks of oil from her neck. "So, you're a bike mechanic now, huh?" he said.

Thoroughly de-oiled, Lissa examined the way her father scrunched up his face, unable to scold her for doing what she'd seen him do. They both knew the power she held over him with her simple downcast gaze and chubby-cheeked smile. These were tricks she couldn't play on her mother.

"Why not? I like the garage," she said, now smiling.

"So it seems." She felt his strong hands lift beneath her armpits and gently place her down in the light. She waited until he gave her the nod that she was all clear.

Over the years, the family's two-car garage had morphed into Michael's workspace. No longer suitable for parking, it was now full of tools and ideas. In the garage she knew he did important things from the way he paced and scratched his head, jotting notes on a rolling whiteboard, working on carpentry projects and grooming his growing collection of racing cycles. Only recently had Lissa taken an interest in this sacred space—an interest that had become more of an obsession after she too became the proud owner of a purple Huffy with tassels on the handlebar. Ever since her first victory lap around the block without training wheels, she'd been terminally curious about everything cycling. When she biked, she felt the wind push against her face, and she pretended she was flying. She wanted to be a professional bicyclist at the time, which her father said was a "mighty fine choice."

She'd asked how the balance on a bicycle worked, how balance worked in general, and why she had suddenly found her own balance, like magic, after trying so hard and failing so often. She asked how the pedals connected to the wheels, and whether each wheel always had the same number of lines (spokes). Her father had answered as best he could, and she liked the way he looked impressed by her questions and was sometimes unprepared for them. She wanted to challenge him the way his students did because he always spoke about them with such respect.

Michael had let Lissa watch him take one of his bikes apart, explaining that the best way to understand how a thing works is to deconstruct it and put it back together. So now, as Lissa examined her favorite overalls, which seemed spared of oil, she resolved to try again tomorrow. Her stomach growled loudly, as though looking down had invited its input.

"Hungry?" her father asked.

She nodded.

"Maybe next month, when you're seven, you can become my assistant, but you're not ready," he said. "You have to watch and learn for now."

"Six is a solid number," Lissa said. "Tomorrow?"

"Six *is* a solid number," he repeated. "To *watch* and *learn*."

Lissa could feel the excitement as she watched her father pull out the jar of peanut butter and two pieces of sourdough to prepare his famous PB&J sandwiches. He was humming now, the way he always did when he was happy, or after averting a potentially painful event, which would've been had Pauline been around, or if the oil caused real damage.

It was at this moment, as Lissa's father reached for two cobalt blue ceramic plates, however, that something looked suddenly off about him. Lissa watched his knees buckle. There was a chill in the room, and she knew he could feel it too. It rushed through her body, then the house. She felt, in that moment, like she could feel what he could—could feel his heart seize. The plates her father was holding shattered before either of them saw them drop. Lissa couldn't move. She watched, wide-eyed, as he took a seat to close his eyes and slow his breath.

"Dad?" she said cautiously.

He blinked his eyes, his hands twitched. He was silently ticking off numbers as a faint voice with an Irish accent arrived in the room and said, simply, *"Whe'r yer goin' you 'ave time. A'least twenty."*

"Twenty what?" Michael said aloud.

"Yeah, what, Nana?" Lissa said. Twenty could mean anything—minutes, hours, days, or years. It could mean events. It wasn't a number that seemed particularly symbolic. It was an ordinary number, a number no one thought about. "Dad?"

He stared at her, apparently surprised that she'd heard Nana's voice, too. "Stay put, honey. I just lost my balance. You, um, heard her?"

"I talk to Nana all the time."

Knitted eyebrows, Lissa's father nodded. "I'll make your sandwich," he said. "Actually, can you straighten up the living room?"

Lissa agreed, not sure if she should mention anything more about the voice. She began fluffing a pillow while keeping her eyes on her father as he swept up ceramic shards. Meanwhile, he seemed healthy enough. The chill in the house was gone. Nana was gone.

Michael had told Lissa stories about her nana, who was his grandmother, her great-grandmother, but they were all familiar. Lissa had always wanted to say, "I know, Dad. Nana told me already." But Nana told her to keep quiet.

Before her failed attempt at becoming a mechanic, Lissa had been at dinner with both her mother and father, and while she picked at her mac and cheese, trying to pretend she wasn't hearing, Nana's dulcet tones reverberated in her ear and, as the humming grew louder, Michael tried to bring up his own conversations with Nana to Pauline. "I've been having these vivid daydreams," he tried to explain. They'd been at the Spaghetti Warehouse. There was a pole in the center of the restaurant, where servers dressed as firefighters would slide with full-sized birthday cakes for celebratory tables. This was not a birthday, and it felt odd to be there, but Lissa loved their mac and cheese and noisy atmosphere. They'd come to this restaurant when Lissa turned three, the year she had her favorite cake, which was the image of a fairy, so just being there felt like a party.

Pauline chuckled as she picked up a piece of bread and examined it for a moment before setting it back down. "You need to lay off the road races for a while—the endorphins are messing up your brain."

"But listen, these moments," he tried to explain. "It's like I'm tuned in to a voice, a family connection. The vivid dreams remind me of Jung's literature."

Pauline managed to roll her eyes without looking up. Lissa chimed in.

"I tune in, too. I hear Nana, too," she said cheerily, then, registering her mother's stern face, shoved a fistful of her father's French fries into her mouth.

Pauline redirected her stony gaze at Michael, then back to Lissa, before changing the subject to something about the neighbors who didn't pick up after their dogs. She had no tolerance for such subjects and hated the idea of what she referred to as "magical thinking." Lissa's share would soon be referred to as an "imaginary friend episode" that was followed by a few visits to a woman named Dr. Bee, who asked Lissa a bunch of questions she didn't want to answer about her feelings.

And around Pauline, they'd never speak of such things again. Her father even went so far later as to blame the "tuned in" comment on the glasses of wine he'd had that night. So Lissa dropped it that day and ever since. While Pauline was a therapist, Michael worked primarily as a researcher, bouncing around from university to university, depending on who offered him the best contract in any given year. He'd published numerous papers and was making a name for himself in the cognitive behavioral research scene, where he was working on innovative therapies using technology. But his more holistic research didn't get published at the same rate as the widely shared meta-analyses that he believed revealed next to nothing about the human mind.

Lissa would find out much later, after discovering some of his old journals, that all it took was the mention of "mysticism" or "holistic perspectives," and he'd receive a rejection or a request for revision from co-workers with a desperate plea for him to send along a more conventional piece about cognitive behavioral therapy and how Maslow's Hierarchy of Needs influences a person's receptivity to talk therapy treatments.

Michael wrote entries about his academic pursuits but also his own experiences, and Lissa would devour the journals as a teenager. Her father's fascination with the esoteric was more than an academic pursuit. He knew that there was more—that he was, in fact, tuned in—but he had no one to discuss such things within academia or even in day-to-day life. Still, on long bike rides, he'd allow his mind to navigate memory and imagination, trying to reconcile the energetic pull he felt toward a belief system that wasn't religious but purely experiential.

According to his journals, it had begun for him when he was a little older than Lissa, around seven, no more than a year after his grandmother died. Michael began to hear her singing or humming while drifting off to sleep, then recounting Irish myths. He'd been afraid to speak to her, sure it would make him crazy, so he just listened. He began to write letters about his day or what confused him about the world and placed them under the pillow as though she were the tooth fairy, wishing he'd been old enough to ask her questions before she passed. Like the tooth fairy, she reciprocated. Only in place of cash, she began answering him in roundabout ways and on her own time, telling him about her corporeal journey to Ellis Island with his father so many years prior, and recounting in detail the struggles she'd endured in order to offer more comfort to her son, and his son.

"Perhaps some aspect of magical thinking could work as a survival mechanism for young children. And possibly, there is something even more to it all. Perhaps the true magical thinking is the idea that we ever truly expire. I won't answer these questions in my lifetime, of course."

He wrote about how he'd recounted these stories to his parents, who marveled at how smart he was to pick up such precise historical details from encyclopedias. As Michael continued to parrot his grandmother's tales, his parents tried to get him in special classes at school and trivia bowl competitions, only to become perplexed when he didn't show impressive academic proficiency. When they entered him into a history quiz competition with a high-dollar prize, he earned the penultimate position, only two points more than the kid who came in last, which eradicated any notion of his genius.

While Michael's father bemoaned the false promise of superior intelligence, his mother decided to invest more time and energy, spending hours reading to her son and helping him with homework, ultimately aiding him in earning respectable grades by college. When she found the letters he'd written his grandmother, which he'd stuffed under his "baby toys" in the closet, she quietly warned him that magical thinking was dangerous before burning each letter in the fireplace to keep his father from finding the evidence. As an adult and a father himself, he still spoke with his grandmother from time to time, writing about how much he was comforted by her thick Irish accent and thicker laugh.

"Jest pay attention. Gefts, erm, like yers are lonesome things," he wrote in quotes. She had warned him of misperceptions that can happen when one sees pieces of the future.

Lissa could smell the peanut butter and felt her mouth water. She watched now as her father cut her sandwich into four equal pieces, the way she liked, and she waited until he offered her the plate.

"Thanks," she said, rushing to the table to deconstruct the sandwich and eat it daintily in eight equal pieces: peanut butter, then jelly, a small bite of each, and repeat. Sometimes she'd eat the bread, sometimes not. Sometimes she'd mash it up into a ball and take a small bite out of it. "Dad, Nana told me to tell you not to worry. Twenty isn't bad. It's not today." she said.

Michael turned around. With two sandwiches on his plate, he sat down at a table he'd made last summer that he often said bothered him—it wasn't stained the right color, and one table leg was slightly short near where he sat at the southeast corner. He took a generous bite of his first sandwich. "Tell me about the voice you heard," he said at last.

"Mary Leigh. Nana. She said don't worry."

"And she said she'd tell you a story?"

"Yep. She always does. I remember the stories you told me, too, but she tells me new ones. She also tells me when she talks to you."

"You know your nana only shows up for us, right?" Michael said, confiding in Lissa. "You have to allow yourself a little magic."

She just smiled and shrugged with the same level of mild interest. "I like it. I'm never alone. I know Mom doesn't like it," she said.

The sound of Pauline's SUV pulling up startled them both. They looked around the kitchen to ensure there was no evidence of the WD-40 incident. Michael put his finger to his lips, then whispered. "You'll have to tell me the stories when she shares them, honey, but let's keep it between you and me?"

Lissa nodded. "Okay. I liked Dr. Bee, but I'd rather hang out with you in the garage on Saturdays."

"Good. Me too. How's your sandwich?"

"Dee-lish!" Lissa said, licking off the last bit of jelly before running to the door to greet her mother with sticky hands.

Pauline hugged Lissa to her left side as she dropped her briefcase and purse on the chair. "Honey," she said, speaking past her daughter. "Dr. Andrews loves your personal health accountability research. I think you have a shot at going to D.C. to present. I hope you don't mind that I shared it."

Lissa watched her father nod with feigned excitement, then he winked at Lissa as her mother bent to kiss her forehead. She knew she would learn more from her father about what only they could see and hear. Nana's voice would stop for far too long, but Lissa always knew she was there.

Ceremony

Unsure what year it was, let alone what day, Lissa sat on the ground, cross-legged in front of the biggest fire she'd ever seen. Glenda, whose hair was whiter than she remembered, and Doreen, who looked the same, were sitting similarly, with eyes closed, reciting a chant so quickly that Lissa couldn't make out the words.

Though the picture of this scene arrived and faded, she could also see Trent in tight jeans and a grass-stained tee, telling her that he was going to move on. He snarled at her, and she vividly saw the look in his eyes when he glanced around, the blood rushing down his legs. She hadn't been there in body, but she still saw it all. She had killed a man who was just trying to get his life together. She had killed a man who she had once loved.

When Trent and Lissa had first started dating, about a month in, he'd arrived at her door in a suit, holding the largest stuffed elephant she'd ever seen. "I wanted to do this at the restaurant tonight, but I can't wait. You are the love of my life. I want you to be the mother of my children." He fell to one knee and smiled that full smile, his heavy-lidded gaze hopeful. "I love you, Lissa."

The ring was lovely, though she could have cared less about such things, and the scene was like something out of a movie. She wanted to press pause on this moment as she took it all in. Still, the question seemed unfair. She was falling in love with Trent, but unsure if she actually loved him yet. The fall was still mid-point. But he seemed perfect. So incredibly handsome and kind, a family man, and supportive of her. He'd listen to her difficulties at work and tell her she was worth more. Just as his smile was beginning to fade, she stopped it.

"Yes."

And things had been good after that, for so many long months. It wasn't until Trent started slipping off the condom and talking about children that Lissa began to suspect that she might have made a mistake. They had spoken of children in abstract, or at least Lissa had, but it suddenly seemed the most important thing to Trent.

He dove into his work, talking more often about the family

he wanted to support, a family that extended beyond the two of them. Lissa, who felt like she had yet to find her calling and still entertained the vague notion of one day owning a business or teaching full-time, said she needed clarity about her life direction before she had children. She was still figuring things out.

It was late on a Tuesday evening when he first hit her. They'd been married for only a few months. The argument hadn't been big or involved. It was a dumb thing, a trivia question that Lissa couldn't remember to this day. Something simple that they didn't agree on. Lissa was sure she was right though, and when she argued, Trent pinned her to the wall and told her to shut up. She said no, and he slapped her. A slap—that's how it began. When the pandemic started, she no longer needed to argue to get pinned to the wall or feel his rough hands on her face or jabbing at her ribs. All she had to do was say the wrong thing.

When the lockdowns began, she knew she would die. He was home too much, and everything she did irritated him—namely, not getting pregnant. "I have a family legacy to pass down. We need to see the doctor."

Lissa went to the appointments he made, grateful for the delays that occurred when hospitals were overrun. She kept a stock of morning after pills buried in a small box beneath the bushes that lined the side of their home. Occasionally, she called a friend with the intention of telling the truth, but that person would inevitably want to talk about the pandemic—everyone was going through so much, and she'd worry that it'd be too much of a burden to confide all she was going through. And Pauline, who hated Trent, would go ballistic. There was a deep belief then that she was not worth more, and so she stayed. She stayed, and he got worse, and she forgot who she was.

Looking back, she realized that there was a certain amount of magic at play even then, how, though muted, her Nana's voice would still sometimes appear as she drifted off to sleep. Lissa had left her body during years of that marriage and left it to fend for itself. The part of her that was truly alive floated above, watching, waiting. And it wasn't until she went to The Lavender Center that it returned to her.

Now, sitting in this circle, she felt the full weight of Trent's inner rage and his inability to see beyond his own self-interest. She felt what he felt—entitlement and fear—and the sensation was like a sludge coating her insides. "Get him out of me," she screamed toward the stars, jarring Glenda and Doreen. Annika sheltered her with a hug.

"Shhhh. He's leaving."

The women cast a circle and explained to Lissa that the only way to reverse a spell like this was to erase the timeline. This would not be easy. Lissa would have to invoke other spirits to purge herself of Trent's presence. She would have to restore his life.

"He'll come back if this is successful?"

"You'll come back to the moment you cast the spell. You'll have the opportunity to begin again—but before you do, you have to experience everything you set into motion."

The four women stood in a circle, and Ash found a low tree to climb and perch in, watching both them and potential prey. Lissa closed her eyes and reached out her hand to Annika and Doreen, who held tight to Glenda. All four could see the scene at a small church in the east of Portland, Indiana. Trent's mother, Lena, sturdy from generations of farmers, stood outside a church, holding a microphone. Her nails were purple, dagger-like.

Trent had once told Lissa that ever since their family had come into money, his mother had started going to the beauty salon twice a week, and his father had started the landscaping business. Aside from her nails and shoes, along with the fact that her hair was always done, even on the most humid summer days, no one could tell the family had money. They liked to live affluently but under the radar, so they stayed in a relatively small and run-down house.

Lena held the mic with the swaying confidence of a preacher and spoke with the same conviction. "When Trent was a kid, we used to tease him. All he ever talked about was being a dad. And, you know, if he would've been a dad, we know he would've set that kid up for greatness. He was the smartest one in our family, building that business up out of nothing. If he would've had his fair shot on this planet, if some monster wouldn't have taken him out so early, we know he would've done things in this world. He would've been a leader in his community. Probably would've run for office or something." She looked off into the distance for a moment, straightening her shoulders.

"Things won't be the same around here without him. And, you know, lil Jimmy, you better fucking step up because I, uh, I don't think your brother is going to look down from heaven and tolerate any of your bullshit. All right, well, that's all I got to say. Love you. Love you, Trent. Rest well, my child."

Lissa, Glenda, Annika, and Doreen watched. The funeral

wasn't long. The whole thing lasted an hour, tops. After a few others spoke, everyone celebrated Trent's life by toasting cans of Pabst Blue Ribbon and throwing hot dogs on the grill. People laughed and cried.

At one point, Trent's mother smiled and excused herself to the bathroom, where she broke down in tears, sobbing and gasping for breath. Lissa squirmed and cried out toward the moon.

"You have to stay in your body!" Glenda demanded. "Stay! Stay in your body!"

Lissa didn't want to; she didn't think she could. She felt as though something were squeezing, pushing her spirit out of her skin. The only thing that kept her grounded was looking to Annika, whose eyes held her, and she could see that her friend was sharing the mental anguish. This was love.

Lissa knew love. She knew a daughter's love, too, and this was the pain she had to feel next. Her mother. Her mother's regret. Her mother's regret for letting her marry Trent, which she couldn't have controlled anyway, but it was an ache. The regret after a lifetime of dedicating herself to trying to save others, only to end up killing one, taking a life. She felt her mother and saw her at home, rocking, like a mad person, like a person who needed her own support, like a person who was too gone to know how to ask. She rocked there, and Lissa heard knocking at the front door, watching in horror as officers busted down the door and rushed her. Her mother was handcuffed. One of the officers didn't see the glasses sitting by her side and crushed them. The green ones, her favorite pair.

Lissa screamed, "I'm sorry, I'm sorry, I'm sorry, I'm sorry, Mom. I'm sorry, I'm sorry, I'm sorry…" She apologized more, squirming, squeezing Annika's hand, realizing it was now her father's hand. "Dad," she said. "What can I do?"

"It's going to be okay. Stay the course," her father's voice said. "You're safe." He started laughing gently, the way he had when she got into the oil that day so many decades ago, the day he received his own sentence. She had to trust that he knew. That he could see that everything would be okay, and this was possible to recover from. She was trying for something new and stumbling through. She had made a mistake, but he was here to cover for her.

"What should I do?" she asked again.

"What you keep forgetting. To trust yourself. Trust your own magic. Trust it all."

"Dad?"

"When you do, you'll realize how formidable my daughter is. *You're unbreakable. You're powerful.*" With this, his voice faded, and Lissa began to feel the full weight of loss she'd felt so many years prior when Pauline told her what had happened, that he'd been found on the side of the road, his bike thrown ten feet behind him.

As Lissa screamed out, the rest of the women continued unphased. The coven called in the spirit of the goddess Brigid, all mighty, all powerful, all seeing. The goddess of poetry, smithcraft, a warrior who arrived and lifted her. They invoked Morrigan, the goddess of death and rebirth, destiny and battle, and Lissa saw the circle expand and all those she'd seen return.

They were all there, and as she looked from her father to these women who had taken her into the very goddesses she'd read about, she felt everything inside of her liquify. Her hand was released, and she collapsed to the ground. The women began to sing. It was a song she wasn't familiar with, but Nana's voice was there, struggling to harmonize, as her father hummed in tune. Cheek to dirt, Lissa felt her body squirm as it regenerated. The singing began to fade out, or she did—she wasn't sure—and time began to skip.

Lissa could hear sounds from childhood: She felt a new rhythm, a wave moving, as though everything was resetting. Scenes from high school, her marriage, TSH, and TLC arrived, then folded over her, leaving quicker than they arrived. She heard someone yell, "Give it all to the earth below. Trust," and she tried.

As the swirl of events continued and the chatter across generations and time began to amplify, Lissa went from feeling as though she wanted to escape her body to feeling a strange sort of neutrality. Her final glimpse of the moment arrived as she pushed herself up to stand and rejoined hands with Annika. She began to sing with the women, not sure how she knew the words, and with her eyes open, everything went dark as time enveloped her.

She heard a horn honk, and a young man's voice calling out. Her body was thrust forward, and she was alone in the backseat of a car. The driver in front of her was swerving, and she felt time unfold.

Lissa, Redux

"Can you hear me? Ma'am?" The driver's young voice cracked.

It took all Lissa's strength to blink her eyes open, to escape the nightmare, but when she did, the driver's worried eyes greeted her. She let the light in and registered his panicked expression, his young face creasing between the brows.

"Are we okay?" she asked.

"I was going to ask *you* that. I didn't know what to do. Can you sit up? Should I call an ambulance or take you to a doctor? We had to get off the road, but I was able to stop the car safely. I think you hit your head."

There was an instant then, a flash of darkness. By the time Lissa slowly allowed the light to arrive, and her eyes flickered, barely able to open again, she wasn't sure what she'd done. The young man dropped her off in front of the Grandview Inn, and she thanked him. "Déjà vu?"

"Huh?" he asked.

It took Lissa a moment to remember where she was going. She saw the lighted sign for Grandview Inn and headed toward it. Everything felt familiar, but also eerily unpredictable. Déjà vu. When the young driver waved and honked, his muffler scraping the street, Lissa nodded. She stood a moment before opening the heavy doors to the restaurant. She was a few minutes early. A server approached her and led her back toward the booth. "Ma'am, your party is waiting. Would you like something to drink?"

"I think I've had enough excitement. Thanks." When Lissa looked over to the booth, she saw her mother sitting with a handsome man whose dark hair was dusted gray around the temples. She'd met him before, right? He wore a short beard and an easy smile. He was laughing.

Before Lissa reached the booth, Pauline turned to her and clapped, then clasped her hands together. "Honey! You look adorable." She leaned in, whispering in her ear, "But the dress would've been nice." Turning to their dinner companion, she announced, "Meet Dr. Cal Gregory."

"You all came here together? I'm confused. We've already met, I mean . . ." Time had reset. Things felt vaguely familiar but not entirely.

Pauline shifted, tilting her head to evaluate her daughter.

"Confusion is a sign of intelligence in a lot of scenarios," Cal said. "Yes, your mother insisted we arrive together."

Dizzy, Lissa excused herself to the bathroom. She held on to the toilet seat as though it were a raft and waited for the shock to ease. When she was finally able to stand, she felt nauseous, almost as though she had a concussion. She wondered if she should sit back down but instead stumbled toward the sink to wash her hands, where she caught her reflection in the mirror.

Her top was stained near the armpits, and her eyes had that puffy look they got after more than one glass of wine. She examined herself, realizing the mirror had a crack in it. As she centered her face, she could see two versions of herself. The one who did as she was told, who showed up where she was expected to and got pushed around by the world. Then, there was the wild woman, the witch.

"The witch," she said, just as another woman entered the bathroom. Lissa didn't care. She had no memory of all that had transpired, but she knew something was off.

Trent had recently been released from prison, and the thought scared her. She worried he'd do something stupid, like show up here and tackle her to the ground. She started a text to Annika but was unsure what to say. She dropped her phone back in her purse instead and returned to the table.

"Since you were late, I took the liberty of ordering you onion soup, no cheese, and a cranberry walnut salad." Pauline informed her upon her return.

"You just got here and already ordered for me? Um … If it's not too late, I'd actually like a Caesar salad instead."

"Oh, honey." Pauline leaned in, whispering to Lissa. "Are you having one of those panic attacks? Do you need to excuse yourself for a while? Your pupils are dilated, and you don't eat Caesar salads, not since the olden days."

Lissa used to order a salmon Caesar salad every time she went to dinner. It was her routine. That and a martini or glass of wine. When she started over, she'd started over completely. New diet, new routines, new way of dressing.

"No, Mom. I'm fine. Or maybe I'm not. Or maybe I'm really great. I don't know." Sliding into the booth, Lissa took a deep breath and tried to ground herself by pushing all four corners of her feet into the carpet below. She heard singing, but it quickly faded. It was as though she'd woken from a dream, but everything was more abstract awake. Another deep breath. "So, Dr. Cal Gregory ..." Lissa started, grasping for some sense of normalcy. "What are you a doctor of?"

"Psychologist. I took over your mother's station and many of her clients, though my research is in other areas."

"Mostly took over," Pauline added.

"True. Your mother just took a call from one of my clients and diffused what could have been a very difficult situation."

"You are welcome. Though Mrs. J would have done just as well speaking to you."

"So . . . No expertise on overbearing, controlling parents?" Lissa asked Cal with a side glance toward Pauline, which Pauline didn't seem to pick up. Another deep breath. She was doing well. "What areas?"

"PTSD and anxiety."

It didn't escape Lissa that Pauline had been trying to get her to see a psychologist for years. "Convenient. Do you ever work with people whose reality splits in half? Like, there are two of them?"

"Borderline personality disorder? Yes." Cal replied, casting a glance at Pauline.

"No. Like people who live in alternate universes."

"It sounds like you mean schizophrenia." Cal shook his head.

"Not my specialty. And like psychosis, it's an umbrella term. In the future, I think what we refer to as schizophrenia now will be at least twenty different diagnoses." He paused. "I seem to be boring you."

"No, not at all." She wondered how the shop was doing. The last thing she remembered, they needed to place an order. Then she got a glimpse of the panic she felt when she heard news of Trent's release. The timeline was readjusting. She remembered her mother's texts, the set-up. It was like the past was filling itself in bit by bit, the missing pieces falling into place.

Her mother's manicured hand squeezed her thigh. Luckily, her nails were squared and dull.

"Oh, sorry. I'm feeling off today. Did Mom tell you what I

do?"

"I told him you were a little into the woo woo stuff," Pauline interrupted, her voice crisp.

Cal laughed kindly. "I respect the woo."

"Well, good, because I'm more than a little woo. I'm ingrained in the spiritual world. I'm pretty sure it saved me. Not that there aren't scientific studies to back up quite a lot of the therapies we offer. And the ones science doesn't back up, science has borrowed from."

"The spiritual world is not exactly a cure-all, obviously," Pauline muttered.

Mercifully, Cal responded, "Yes, your mother told me you owned a business. That takes a lot of courage. I'm intrigued."

Lissa smiled, remembering the business challenges, Ash. "Thanks. It was a big move. Things were tough for a time, but they're getting better. It seemed for a few years there, people were more inclined to let robots or apps tell them exactly what their diet and medication regime. You should swing by."

"What services do you offer?"

"Tarot. I can also give you a reading. I can correspond with any deceased relatives or spirit guides."

"My spirit guides, eh? Yeah, the therapy bots and spirit guides don't get along, I'm sure."

"Don't feel bad," Lissa shook her head. "Most people think it's ridiculous. Or they want others to think they think it's ridiculous." Lissa glanced over at her mother, who looked both taken aback and a little impressed.

"No, it's not that. You've intrigued me. I'm down for whatever kind of reading. One thing I learned along the way is not to discount anything I haven't investigated for myself. You know, I feel partly responsible for that tech because I helped early on when we didn't see the full picture. I remember when they first rolled out, the huge dip in traditional therapy for a while, too. Remember that, Pauline?" Cal said.

"It didn't really impact my list of clients, but I was on my way to retirement by then. You were still building up your list. I personally love my app, but I see what you mean."

"It was just coming on as you left, you're right. I just remember doubting myself during the craze. I worried I didn't have the ability to truly help people. After a few years, my professional option is that that technology for treatment is worse than no tech at all. RoboHealth sucks. And again, that's just a professional opinion." Lissa laughed.

"Do you have an opening tomorrow?" he asked. His eyes, the deepest blue she'd ever seen, held genuine interest. She saw herself in them.

In that moment, it was as though she was no longer watching a movie of herself, but actually present. They stared at each other for a moment before she answered. *What would he think of her a month from now? A year? Would she look less like a person and more like an object to slice open at his whim?* Anxiety asked. Then something else chimed in. *And if he does, he better watch out.*

"If so, I'm there. I have all day," he said as Lissa calibrated. *I am formidable, unbreakable* … "Great. Swing by any time after 11."

Lissa knew she'd have to work through some lingering anxiety, but as she sat in that booth, she felt more herself than she remembered feeling in years. She was still reconciling in her mind what was real and what wasn't. Trent might still be out there, maybe not. Maybe she'd dreamed it all. Whatever the case, she'd face the reality of the situation squarely. And she'd trust.

When the three of them parted ways for the evening, Lissa stuck out her hand to shake Cal's, and she noticed the brightness in his smile, the subtle bow as he said goodnight, and nodded to her mother as he walked away. "I feel like I already know him, Mom. Like we're good friends."

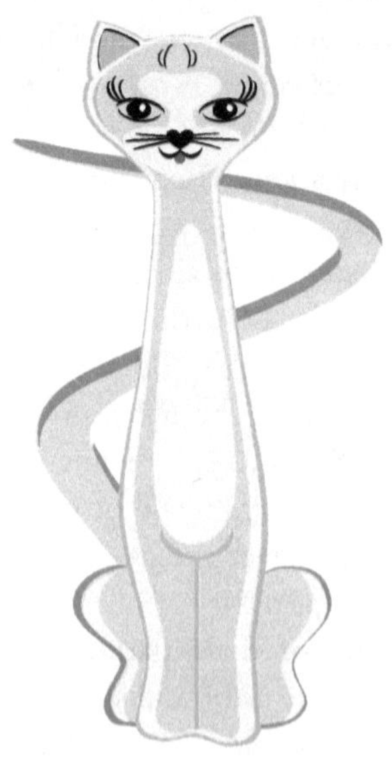

Ash

Monday, February 5 (6:30 a.m.)

The pawn shop Lee had purchased lost power a few days after he cleared the inventory, and when the electrician said the building was a fire hazard waiting to happen, Lee began to panic after analyzing the renovations that would've cost more than he could have invested. Though he'd been stoic about it, Pauline knew it broke his heart, and she began to research law firms that could represent him against the seller.

"You don't have to get involved, Paulie," Lee said.

Pauline caught him in a gaze she intended as paralyzing. "This is what I do well. I fix things."

"I feel like an idiot. Everyone is starting businesses with these incentives, but I might just not be cut out to make it work. I couldn't handle business school. I don't think like that. I tried to open a food truck a few years ago, and that was a disaster."

"You're just too trusting, and you need a partner," Pauline told him, smiling, checking her lipstick in her cell reflection.

"A partner?" He raised an eyebrow at her.

It didn't take long to reveal that the previous owner had a relationship with the building inspector and a history of questionable business practices, which would not look good for him in court, and he knew it. When a few phone calls prompted a quick settlement, Lee let the place go. His version of processing defeat involved an inordinate amount of silence and steadiness that Pauline knew was embarrassment. She told him not to give up, he had the funds, but she never expected his new plans to take her back to The Grandview Inn, which he'd bought at auction after the owners filed for bankruptcy earlier that year. Pauline was thrilled.

"You are unbelievably perfect. Who knew I'd pick up the perfect man at a pawn shop?" She smiled at him.

"Life pays when you improvise." He reached across the table to give her hand a squeeze. "Besides, you're likely going to run the place. I just want to cook."

"Damn right. Let's not improvise on this," she said. The two drank a bottle of wine and charted out rough plans for the restaurant and, for the first time since Michael died, Pauline felt a kind of hope for the future that was nothing short of exhilarating. "We're going to be business partners."

"I think we're more than that," Lee said.

"As much as I loved that restaurant when I was a kid, I always wanted to redecorate. It was outdated even then! I can't wait till we can get started. I do want to keep the bathtub though, or install a new one and paint it silver," Pauline had said at the walk-through, trying to cover up her nerves. What if this venture compromised her relationship with Lee? What if their relationship failed, and they stopped speaking altogether?

When Pauline was a child, she dreamed she'd one day be a scientist, and while she ended up becoming a well-respected researcher and teacher, highly esteemed in certain academic circles, she always felt the lack of physicality and texture in her work. So much was theory, and, as she was always the first to admit, more about highlighting how little is known about the human brain than anything else.

"We know that human beings are resilient, and according to studies around brain plasticity there is great potential to tap this resilience with intention and commitment, but we also know that the human brain is fragile. To find perfect equilibrium in an average life is impossible, and to have any semblance of equilibrium knocked off balance due to an injury or trauma is not unlikely." She'd gone on and on about such things in lecture halls, until she grew too frustrated with other researchers' tendencies to pad their findings with self-improvement messages that got them six-figure book deals and destroyed their intellectual curiosity.

"We all have hard days, but when we have recurring moments of feeling incapable or unmotivated, we need to address the paralyzing forces. I think I might be there in some ways," Pauline told Lee from across the kitchen island.

"Not everyone. Not me," he said, smiling.

"Well, everyone except you, of course. You are perfectly calibrated, always."

"Indeed." Lee was dicing onions, moving fast enough that Pauline was almost certain he was showing off. What if he took off a finger trying to impress her? "But since you are a mere mortal, why not tell me what you mean?"

"It used to drive me nuts when psychologists would smother patients with vague statements and mindfulness practices that were about as useful as prescribing gardening. I mean, it can be useful, but the person has to be in the right place to practice, and that's just the problem. Anyway, what pissed me off more were the therapists who weren't allowing people to own their emotions—to feel the uncomfortable stuff. To be uncomfortable is to grow, a lot of times."

"I can testify to that," Lee said, using the back of the knife to guide the onions from the cutting board into a skillet. "But what about you?"

"And sometimes it's not rational at all," she continued, as though speaking to a class. "We can get sad over false narratives, or angry about things that don't even make sense." She opened a file called TGCAdventure.doc.

"And what about you?" Lee repeated.

"I'm happy. But joy … I mean, hope … it feels strange. So strange that when I have moments when that heavy sense of guilt returns, or that emptiness I lived with for years arrives, the contrast almost knocks me over. You remember that gun I bought from you when you were getting rid of inventory for the previous owner?"

"I do. You terrified me. I thought you were in a gang."

"Hush!" Taking off her glasses and rubbing the bridge of her nose, Pauline examined Lee after blinking a few times. She could see him perfectly, since all her frames were just fashion lenses, and she thought about whether she should actually tell him what she was thinking.

"I'm hushed, I'm hushed" he joked, holding out his hands. "Go on. Irrationality upsets you, and you don't have tolerance for your own," he said.

"Well, yeah! I had these nightmares after I bought that gun. That's why I returned it. There was one recurring nightmare, but it'd come even when I was awake and going about my day, like a flash. I'd get this wave of sensation, this sinking guilt—I felt like I'd actually killed Trent, Lissa's ex. I had a memory of it. I shot him in the lower back, watched him bleed out. It wasn't clean, like a movie; it was gritty and loud. But what's worse is that I remember his eyes. Seeing his eyes as he turned around in disbelief. I couldn't look away. He had this childlike look of innocence. I could see every redeeming quality about him in his face, then he lost that flicker of life. It wasn't just the monster that was dying. It was also the little boy inside him. That light."

"Hm."

"That's all you have? Hm?"

"Well that's dark, but I don't think it makes you crazy" he replied matter-of-factly. "You wanted to defend your daughter, and you were probably preparing for the worst-case scenario. So much so that you dreamed about it vividly, which gave you a sense of a memory."

"But—it's so real every time," she urged. "The way the birdsong around us stopped, the way his shirt began to suck into his body as it saturated with blood. I've had vivid dreams before. I used to take sleeping pills that gave me wild dreams, but nothing this lifelike."

"Did any of your clients ever have anything like that?" He stirred the contents of the skillet with a wooden spoon.

"Dreams were not my thing. I never got much into Jung or anything like that. It all felt so abstract. I think you're right, though. It was like a preparation in my mind, in case. Thank goodness that guy stayed the hell away from us."

"Can I do anything? I mean, can I help?"

"No. I didn't want to bother you with it. I've been talking to my own therapist about it, but you're better. You should bill out at $300 an hour."

"Well, if this little venture doesn't work out, I might just do that."

"It'll work out." Pauline said.

"I hope so. Have you looked him up, lately?" Lee asked, as though already knowing the answer. He flicked some water into a pan and watched it sizzle.

"Regularly. He was in prison again a few months ago. Beat up a customer who refused to pay him on-time, but then he posted about writing a book and self-publishing it, and I think it's actually selling, which goes to prove my point. He'll probably go into politics next, so watch your ballots."

Lee nodded. "Sounds about right. Seems like he's moved on, though. That must give you some peace of mind."

"I hate that the guy's haunting me like this."

"Look, I hear you, but you'll heal. You know this. And I also think that you need to try this so I can know whether to put it on my menu. It's for the brunch menu. Baked Havarti cheese-onion omelet, with sourdough breadcrumbs and fennel."

"That does not sound Midwestern enough for this neighborhood, Lee. Try two eggs over easy and hashbrowns with white toast. Add some black pepper if you want to take a risk." She reached over the counter to bite from his fork and didn't say anything for a long time. "Well now, that tastes like—can I have the rest of that?"

Lee dusted off his hands and smiled. "Bingo. And it's inexpensive. I mean, I have to sell enough of them to warrant the fennel."

As Pauline let the Havarti cheese and onion omelet with caramelized bits settle on her tongue, she allowed her eyes to close and savored the moment. This was as much joy as she'd felt in years. Knowing that Lissa was no longer in danger meant that she could finally dive into her own life again. Granted, the girl still needed to watch all that sugar she ate, and she still had a questionable lifestyle. Oh, and she'd have to get more regular mammograms because breast cancer ran in the family and Lissa was getting to that age. There was still plenty of worry, but it felt like ordinary maternal worry. Nonetheless, the nightmares and brief flashes of guilt hit her, and she had to find strength to stay upright and move forward. She wondered how inappropriate it would feel to Cal to work her into his schedule since her own therapist seemed to only listen and nod. There was nothing harder than finding a good therapist when you'd been one yourself.

"Are you still with me, Paulie?" Lee asked.

"Yeah. Caught up here," she said, tapping her temple. "Maybe this restaurant will be a good way to retire."

"You are going to regret it if you think this'll be a retirement."

"I need to keep myself busy, my friend. I mean, I have a lot of energy, and food is like science. What you did there with a simple onion and butter and some dried-out bread … that's amazing. And I want to learn. Or at least, be close to the kitchen at all times."

"Friend?" he said, rushing around to get within an inch of her.   "I thought we were more than that."

"Partner," she corrected.

He reached for her glasses and gently put them on. "Let's get back to work now. We need this menu complete."

"Don't stretch out the frames. They get stuck like that." As she stood still, allowing Lee to return the glasses to her face, Pauline glanced down at the small plate. "You know, it's ironic. My daughter used to hide my food under the table or feed it to our dog when she was little. Such an honest girl, but when it came to dinner—my cooking, that is—she would do anything to deceive me."

"So you've told me. Look, let's just take it slow. Start with that pan and that stick of butter. We're going to fry some red potatoes. It'll be your signature dish. Paulie's Potatoes."

"Yeah, you wait to see what they taste like first," she said. "And we're not calling it that."

An hour and three attempts later, the two of them decided she'd take care of the décor and help the manager with the front of the house instead.

"Maybe a signature drink would be more appropriate. Speaking of which, I need to invite my daughter to the grand opening," Pauline said.

"Do you think she digs me?" Lee asked. The two had met one time at a charity event for local businesses two months ago. Annika had been presenting on the healing modalities TSH offered as part of a community wellness initiative, and Lee was Pauline's guest. The three of them sat at a round table with catered spaghetti and garlic bread in front of them, and Lissa made a comment about how expressive Lee's face was after he took a bite.

"It's like they threw canned tomato soup on some noodles," he'd said too loud, and one of the catering workers lifted an eyebrow. When he raised his glass to the scowling worker, he looked away and Lissa laughed.

"Food snob much?" she'd asked with a smile.

"The worst kind. Let me tell you about what makes a good sauce. It's all about consistency and the right spices. They have to be understated, but basil is not negotiable." As he started recounting the history of a particular type of tomato that was found in a small Ohio town east of Columbus, Pauline saw the way her daughter's face shifted from wary discomfort to mild acceptance.

"She loves you. Oh, and she says you're surrounded by angels, whatever that means. The girl gets weirder and weirder, but I'm just happy she's happy. Happy, and safe." Pauline rushed to her phone and sent Lissa four texts and a video that told her all about the grand opening, what time to be there, what to wear and who all to invite, then swiped through the notifications from her RoboHealth app that told her to eat more dark green vegetables today before bed and take a Vitamin C chew with a magnesium pill. It went on for a page and a half, which she began to skim.

"You might want to delete that thing," Lee said as he began scrubbing one of the pans that held a scalded and failed attempt at fried potatoes. "Check it out." He slid his phone toward her, revealing the top news story about a massive data breach the company was facing. "They're recommending all owners send back the robots and remove the apps, too, for their own safety."

"Is that what this little exclamation point means in the corner?"

"Not only did the hackers steal health and other private information, apparently they hacked the cameras and microphones. Some of the footage is said to be circulating around the dark web. It's a mess. A big story."

"Lissa predicted this a while ago. I thought she was just mad she was losing business."

In true Lissa style, her text response arrived as soon as her name was spoken. It was abrupt. *I'll be there, Mom. And I'll wear what I want.*

Pauline was about to offer some more directives, at least bring that new purse she'd bought her from Loft, but as she began to write something in return, something stopped her. She read her daughter's text again. It was clear. *The girl would wear what she wants. As well you should, Lissa. As well we all should.*

Pauline deleted her RoboHealth app and forwarded her daughter the story with the best emoji she could find to express what she couldn't bring herself to type: "You told me so."

Lissa

Lissa approached the glass doors in a heavy coat lined with faux fur. Her hood was large and sheltered her eyes almost too well. An early snow dusted her shoulders and the sidewalk beneath her. She used her forearm to wipe off the lettering on TSH's large display window, admiring the various crystals, drums, and jewelry displays that showed off their new winter inventory.

After being up all night, completing a ritual spell she'd studied for almost a year, Lissa was surprised she didn't feel tired. She couldn't help but smile as she opened the door, the way she did every day, inviting the bite of the newly chilled winter air to enter and cleanse the space. *Our healing space.*

Just as she was about to unlock the door, a man cleared his throat behind her. She turned to see a shadowy figure, also hooded, half a block away but moving quickly with something erratic about his step. Lissa felt her heart pound as she scrambled to open the door, but then as the snow fell on her exposed wrists, she felt something cool throughout her body.

She turned the key in the lock but looked back and saw the figure coming toward her. Instead of rushing inside, she put up her palm in such a way that it could've been mistaken for a simple wave. She felt her heart energy swell at the center point of her hand and silently called to the women who reminded her who she was. She felt her own fire inside swelling, expanding, and she removed her hood. And he came into the light. He was older, a bit wild-eyed and feral, and he appeared to be in pain.

"Can I help you?" Lissa asked him, her hand still up. Her voice smooth.

He stopped walking, then sharply turned away and rushed toward the bus stop, muttering to himself. Lissa kept her hand up and watched as he turned back around and something in him softened, if just for a moment.

Once inside, Lissa shed her coat and smiled. A full smile. All the inventory at the new shop came from local vendors now, which cut down on costs. Raven was a full-time employee and desperately in love with the redhead who had magically influenced him to take regular showers and show up relatively close to being on time. He was pulling longer shifts before taking a short vacation so had closed last night and would be back in soon. Lately, he not only showed up when and where he said he would, but he left the place in pristine condition.

So long as he was able to take time to go on meditation retreats with his new girlfriend, Raven was accountable—and, it turned out, an incredible salesperson. He had a way with the wealthier seekers who frequented the store. Perhaps because he offered a persona they were looking for. Many of the people he met on his outings were vendors of some sort, which allowed Lissa and Annika to support other small businesses, not to mention offer benefits to their growing staff.

Now that they were out of O'Malley's place, both Lissa and Annika had their own rooms to meet with clients, and there was a common space for yoga instructors and practitioners of various healing modalities to host classes. Between renting out space and selling their services and products, their profit margins were soaring, and everything felt sustainable. Sure, there were better and worse days, and the wellness robots were full of new promises—the latest commercial promised it could interpret dreams—but the witches offered what no one else could.

Lissa noticed Annika's kombucha bottle left beneath the counter. She entered the security code. As she did every day, she began to walk the perimeter of the store, blessing the product and the makers alike. She bowed to the section of the store that held sculptures of worldly deities and ceremoniously dusted the floor with salt, which she swept from the back of the store to the front to clean and clear any negative energy from the day before. Soft ambient music filled the air.

Lissa scanned the store for spaces that needed replenishing or dusting as she listened to the shop's email messages, which were read in the sender's voice unless they were spam. Most of the messages were salespeople, so she was jarred to hear a message from Glenda. "Doreen and I just wanted to send a message to say hello. We'll be stopping by soon with offerings for your new space. Blessed be," she said.

"Play again," Lissa told her smart device. She played it twice more, before scanning the store. "They know everything."

She tuned into the space and scanned for spirits, hearing only the humming of Nana, which had become a soundtrack for Lissa's life, which warmed any room and settled any nerves. While she couldn't hear him, she felt the presence of her father's stories all around. One of the sculpture artists who had his own shop a few blocks away had sold Lissa a colorful sculpture of overlapping painted bicycle wheels that reminded her of her father. She would meditate on them most mornings, and today, she sat to do the same before hearing a gentle knock against the glass, so gentle in fact that she barely heard it.

Unlocking the door, she let Cal in and greeted him with a hug. "I could barely hear your knock. You knock with the strength of a toddler," she told him.

"Part of my charm." He embraced Lissa. The two had been friends for a year now, never quite connecting in the way Pauline had hoped, and part of it was the perpetual awkwardness between them, which they liked to laugh about. Meanwhile, Cal had enjoyed his reading so much that shortly after first connecting to his spirit guides, he became fascinated by spirituality and the unpublished writings of Lissa's father. He'd even begun a rigorous meditation training and was practicing teaching at TSH. "You're early for class. I have you on the schedule for ten," she said.

"Annika or Raven here yet?"

"No, I think Annika might take the day off. She felt a little under the weather this morning," Lissa said, again, trying not to smile, which might come off as a bit sadistic. Annika had been getting migraines ever since Ash disappeared. She said she might have an allergy to him *not* being around, but Lissa knew better. She'd stopped by to check on her friend that morning and had draped Annika's forehead with a warm cloth, reminding her to breathe, that she had to trust it'd all be okay. Annika had given her a curious look. You sure have changed.

"Too bad. Means you can't take my class," Cal said. He glanced at some of the new crystals. "What's that smell, Frankincense?"

"Indeed. And lavender. Good nose. Look on the bright side. I'll join your class Saturday," Lissa said. "Since you're here, I think I'll open a little early."

Cal nodded. "Sounds good. I have a few clients meeting me here today. Hopefully, some new business for you," he said.

"Wonderful," Lissa said. "Thanks for helping Mom with those nightmares, by the way. You've been a godsend."

"I am not at liberty to talk about that." He held up his palm towards her, his eyes smiling. "HIPPA."

Lissa laughed. Just as she unlocked the door and flipped the sign to OPEN, Raven wedged himself inside, appearing out of nowhere.

"Thirty seconds to spare!" he announced. "I brought gifts." He held up a brown bag full of bagels as Lissa erected the sign that requested all electronic devices be turned off before entering the shop. Then she did the same, storing her phone in a safe near the register and calling for the men to do so as well.

She watched as Cal sat on a meditation cushion, checking himself out in the mirrored wall, angling his body this way and that way. She wished him love. He'd been on so many bad dates in this last year. Seemed to have a thing for narcissists, but he'd remained sweet. Cal had helped Pauline work through many panicked nights since time reversed. It was as though she'd kept some of the guilt that came from the alternative action, and she still refused most of Lissa's offerings as "too new agey."

Cal rubbed his hands together and closed his eyes, held his hands to heart. He'd also helped Lissa work through a complex set of all-too-human emotions when her mother revealed that she was dating a pawn shop owner who was planning to open a café in the neighborhood. She had needed time before she was ready to meet Lee, and Pauline gave her this grace, till the two went into business together. Though there were no red flags, and Lee came across as one of the humblest people Lissa had ever met, but she still couldn't help but think about her father every time she looked at them. It was a process that Cal helped her reconcile. Meanwhile, Annika gave her a hard time about the petty thoughts that would slip through.

In exchange for Cal's generosity, Lissa blessed him daily. She and Annika had taught him about connecting with nature, various crystals, and even shared with him some extremely basic spells. He seemed naturally inclined to seek and though he drew the line at certain things, his respect for the craft was genuine. Although they ran the store, Lissa and Annika knew enough to keep their practice to themselves with most people in this town. At least for now.

Cal glanced back at the room. "It's so funny. I still get nervous. I never get nervous with therapy, but I worry what people will think sometimes. Some of these clients have never so much as meditated or practiced contemplation for more than a few minutes. One guy even dropped me when I suggested he attend an in-person mindfulness

Though a part of her wanted to think otherwise, Lissa agreed.

The shop had and would continue to see protests. It'd been vandalized a few times, too, especially around elections, but TSH carried on, using each event as an opportunity to call the local news and get their name out there a little more. Business always picked up.

"I get nervous, I think, because it's not clinical. I'm sharing something personal."

"You're sharing your practice. Think of it this way: mindfulness, like magic, is just the intentional direction of energy," she told him, as Annika had told her years ago. "It's never manipulation, so you don't have to worry about anyone else's reactions or actions."

"Thanks, Dr. Williams Jr. Let me know if you two need help with anything. I'm going to start coffee in the back," Cal said, kissing Lissa's cheek.

"You practice being cool, man. We got you," Raven said. The two men exchanged an awkward glance. They didn't dislike each other, but they didn't quite get along either.

When Annika arrived at the store a few hours later, Lissa wasn't surprised. She didn't look like herself though. No alert gaze, no attitude. She just arrived like anyone else. The store had a few people wandering the aisles, and one of the regulars, Tammy, was humming along to a tune that was most definitely not what was playing overhead.

"What are you doing here? Feeling better?"

When Lissa looked in Annika's eyes, she saw concern. "It happened," Annika whispered.

"What?" Lissa whispered back, trying to hold back her knowing smile.

"I don't know if it'll last, but ..." She paused as though listening for something beyond the music and homed in on a few of the customers, then Lissa. "I think Inga's spell wore off. Or I was able to finally reverse it. I can't hear anyone, any thoughts, unless I try. It was like my body went through this big purge this morning, then suddenly, it was all clear. My mind was clear."

Lissa intentionally thought Annika needs to stop it already with the late-90s eye makeup, but Annika just kept looking ahead, unfazed. She truly couldn't hear.

"It's like Inga's grip on me has released. I think it might've happened at our last ceremony, or maybe it just happened. I can't even remember what it was like to hear so many voices in my head." She smiled wistfully. "Unfortunately though, that's not my only news."

Lissa stood back, thinking about Glenda's message and wondering if Annika would ever figure out it was her. "Spill."

"Andrea said she saw a cat on the side of Summit Street that looked like Ash. She called animal control because he was severely injured."

Just as Lissa was about to sit to offer a moment of silence, Tammy hollered, "Lissa, I'd like an akashic reading. Maybe tomorrow afternoon?" She was wearing a zebra striped blazer and holding her winter coat, which was the shiniest pink Lissa had ever seen. "This girl is gifted. She talks to the dead and tells them what's what," Tammy informed a woman who was cautiously exploring the gift book section.

"Of course, just let me know when you're ready to schedule," she told Tammy, who had been visiting Lissa regularly since they met. Her son had moved into the afterlife after a contentious but heartfelt exchange. Now, Tammy was looking to find her soulmate. She was what Annika referred to as a spiritual hanger-on.

Lissa turned to Annika. She hadn't seen or tuned into Ash at all, and as Tammy had hollered, her gift truly was to connect with those who were transitioning out of this world. When there was no contact, it meant the soul's mission and message was complete. She was learning to trust this, and she knew the cat was Lissa's familiar.

"Ash did his work here," Lissa said. "You both did everything you could, and I thank you."

Annika became still. "You knew? I was beginning to suspect. You've been so different lately," she said.

"I know now."

"Warrior," Annika said, playfully punching her friend in the arm.

Since the timeline shift, Lissa had felt waves of anxiety arrive, ebbing and flowing, but over time, she learned to work with them consciously, to use them as fuel. For all the ill-intent Inga may have had, she'd been right about the way Lissa's anxiety could interrupt the magic that made her, so she learned to channel it. When worry would rush her, crashing inside when she'd look up or out the window and get a glimpse of Trent coming toward her or glaring from the window, she'd reorient and see her own reflection. Every day, remembering her strength became more automatic and her magic stronger.

Over the years, not only could she tune in to those in other realms, but she learned to listen to the voice that she'd abandoned some time in young adulthood, the voice that didn't question or trust others over herself. She finally felt as though she could be here for those who had protected her these years, and when she saw what the coven was capable of, she began reversing Inga's spell over Annika.

"Check that out, ladies!" The two women walked to the window, Lissa leading Annika by the hand, instead of the other way around, and the two of them looked out at the big, fat snowflakes gracefully falling on their tree-lined street. It felt as though they were inside of a snow globe.

When Lissa caught sight of a couple walking across the street, she felt an immediate tug. The woman's shoulders slumped, and his were rigid. He snapped his head towards the woman and said something that seemed to deflate her all the more. Lissa could see the rage he was emitting and thought about the warning. Closing her eyes, she concentrated.

"Oops," Annika said, trying to stifle a chuckle. "That was like a cartoon fall."

When Lissa opened them again, the man was on the ground, face down in a pile of icy snow. The woman was helping him up, but when he scrambled to his feet, he fell again. Lissa wanted to do more, but she couldn't. Her friend grabbed her hand

"We're where we're supposed to be, Annika said, squeezing.

Lissa traced the scar from her ear to collar bone with her other hand and felt the binding strength of resilience as tiny silver-white snowflakes began to fall, nourishing the earth. She wished the woman well and surrendered to the natural beauty all around. In so doing, she surrendered to herself and those who loved and supported her in whatever ways they could. She resolved to do this every day. Every single day she had left. Because *this* was alchemy.

Acknowledgments

This book was incredibly fun to write. I did most of the drafting at the Rockvale Writers' Colony, and I wanted to thank Sandy Coomer for creating such a sacred space there. It is only with focus and time that I can work on longform projects, and Rockvale gave me that. Moreover, I've met many lovely and interesting people in my time there, and I hope to return. Thank you also to the Ohio Arts Council and the Greater Columbus Arts Council for support of my writing. I want to thank Jen Michalski and Annie Mydla for their support as I began to shape the story, and Ashley Holloway for her friendship and attention to my words in the manuscript's final stages. Thank you to Suzanne Warfield for being a rockstar audio partner and friend. Thank you to my husband, Chris, for designing this beautiful cover, and to Tony Burnett for being such a true partner along this book's journey to print.